Robert Tannahill

Complete Songs and Poems of Robert Tannahill

With Life and Notes

Robert Tannahill

Complete Songs and Poems of Robert Tannahill
With Life and Notes

ISBN/EAN: 9783337179359

Printed in Europe, USA, Canada, Australia, Japan

Cover: Foto ©Andreas Hilbeck / pixelio.de

More available books at **www.hansebooks.com**

Robert Tannahill

COMPLETE SONGS AND POEMS

OF

Robert Tannahill,

WITH LIFE AND NOTES.

TANNAHILL'S BIRTHPLACE.

PAISLEY:

PUBLISHED BY WM. WILSON, Bookseller and Stationer.

1877.

Life of Robert Tannahill.

ROBERT TANNAHILL was born in Paisley on the 3rd of June, 1774. The Cottage, No. 32 Castle Street, is now, from very conclusive evidence, believed to be the birth-place of the poet; and on the anniversary of his birth, 3rd June, 1872, a memorial stone inserted in the front of the building (largely through the instrumentality of the late Bailie J. J. Lamb) was unveiled by Provost Murray in presence of the Tannahill Club, and a large concourse of people. The following is the inscription upon the tablet :—

BIRTH PLACE

OF

ROBERT TANNAHILL,

BORN 3RD JUNE, 1774.

" Here nature first waked me to rapture and love,
And taught me, her beauties to sing."

His father was a James Tannahill, who came originally from Kilmarnock, and his mother, Janet Pollock, the daughter of a farmer near Beith. Both parents were of most respectable character; and his mother, in particular, was gifted with an intelligence above her station. He was the fourth of a family of seven, and his education was very elementary, being limited to the three "R's," and in these even his advancement was not great. The education, however, of one who is born a poet, does not altogether depend on schools and schoolmasters. Even in his school-days he showed a love for verse writing. When only ten years of age Tannahill began the writing of short pieces in verse, which were generally composed upon some "queer" character living in the neighbourhood, or upon some rare circumstance which had taken place. After leaving school he was apprenticed for five years to the hand-loom weaving, and it was while sitting at his loom that the greater part of his pieces were composed. That his literary pursuits might not encroach on his daily occupations, he had a small

rough plank board attached to the side of his loom which
he used as a writing desk ; so that when he had a verse
composed he could jot it down without waste of much time.
In this way, it is said, some of his best songs were composed. With the exception of a short residence in Lochwinnoch (where Alexander Wilson the poet and ornitho-
logist was then too weaving), and two years in Bolton,
Lancashire, his life was spent in Paisley. He and his
brother went to England, tempted perhaps by the report of
great wages given beyond the Border for figured work, for
which Paisley was then justly noted, or more probably by
a desire to see the country. The sudden and serious illness
of his father recalled him to Paisley where he ever afterwards resided, living with, and dutifully supporting his
widowed mother.

Although he doubtless composed many pieces in his
younger days, none of them, with the exception of a song
in praise of Ferguslie Wood, where he used frequently to
wander, were printed. Soon after his return from England the poet had the good fortune to become acquainted
with R. A. Smith, the well-known composer of music,
(also a Paisley man, and then leader of psalmody in the
Abbey),* who composed original music for many of his
songs, while various others he set to music ; and so beautifully do the words and the music suit one another, that
Tannahill and Smith, as household words, go together.

By the advice of Mr. Smith, and other friends, Tannahill published the first edition of his poems in 1807. He
superintended it himself, and occasionally gave the printer's
Devil a shilling to push on the work. It was dedicated to
his bosom friend, William M'Laren, in these terms :—

"To Mr. William M'Laren,
      Sir,
With gratitude I reflect on the happy hours we have
spent together, and in testimony of the high regard I en-
tertain for your many worthy and amiable qualities, I take

---

* A magnificent organ has lately been placed in the Abbey Church,
several fine memorial windows have replaced the old plain glass ones, and
the old houses forming the east side of Abbey Close have been removed,
and a fine wide street formed, thus improving that locality, and exposing
to view the venerable pile.

the liberty of inscribing to you this little volume. Several of the pieces contained in it you have already seen, and if the others afford you any pleasure, it will add much to the happiness of,

Dear Sir,

With true respect and sincerity,

Your friend,

ROBERT TANNAHILL."

The following is the very modest preface of this same edition :—

"The author of the following poems, from a hope that they possess some little merit, has ventured to publish them ; yet, fully sensible of that blinding partiality with which writers are apt to view their own productions, he offers them to the public with unfeigned diffidence. When the man of taste and discrimination reads them, he will, no doubt, find many passages that might have been better, but his censures may be qualified with the remembrance that they are the effusions of an unlettered mechanic, whose hopes, as a poet, extend no further than to be reckoned respectable among the minor bards of his country.

Several of the songs have been honoured with original music by Mr. Ross, of Aberdeen, and others by Mr. Smith, Paisley ; the remainder were mostly written to suit favourite Scotch and Gaelic airs that particularly pleased the Author's fancy.

The "Interlude" was undertaken by desire of the late Mr. Archibald Pollock, comedian, but, alas ! ere it was well begun, his last act was played. He was a worthy man, and died deeply regretted by all who knew him.

The author returns his sincere thanks to his numerous subscribers, particularly to those friends who have so warmly interested themselves in promoting the present publication, and with a due sense of their favours, he has only further to solicit their indulgence in the perusal of his volume, assuring them that their kindness in the present instance, shall long be felt with gratitude and ever esteemed among the first pleasures of the memory. . ..

THE AUTHOR."

The little volume was well received, many of his songs becoming highly popular. Tannahill, however, was not puffed up, but on the contrary asserted that the work had many imperfections. "I am confident," said he, "had I waited a few years longer, I would have presented a volume less exceptionable." He therefore soon set about correcting his productions, and frequently adding a new piece, with a view to a fresh issue. *Love* and *Nature* were his subjects. The former he looked upon with the eye of a poet, and described her features with fidelity, beauty, and grace. His ready access at all times to the " Bonnie Woods of Craigielea," to the " Newton Wood, the " Birks o' Stanley Shaw," and the " Gleniffer Braes," afforded him many advantages in pourtraying so beautifully and truthfully rural scenery.

Some of the fair objects of his love strains are supposed to have been imaginary, yet, in most cases they were drawn from originals. Being well acquainted with the tender feelings of love and domestic attachment, as well as with the manners and customs of the people of Scotland, his verses not only gave great pleasure to the reader, but sank deep into the heart, and were calculated, far beyond any other means to give a perfect picture of the scenes and characters they described. In Tannahill's poetry, imagination is seldom employed to interest the feelings ; but his pictures are drawn from real life, hence the easy access his verses have to the heart. " And in no case does he overstep the limits of delicacy, or express a sentiment offensive to the ear of modesty." It would not, indeed, be any easy task to give the merits of one like Tannahill, who, while earning his daily bread, by hard manual labour, has attained a position, inferior to few of the bards of our country.

The success which the first publication of his poems and songs obtained, made his acquaintance courted by many who were his superiors in station ; and it is gratifying to know that the poet lived to witness the extensive popularity of his songs, which were pronounced to be " the very perfection of song writing," and to hear them sung, both in cottage and in hall.

But his mind, which was naturally prone to despondency, and despairing of ever being able to raise himself above the obscurity of his original condition, soon gave way to a habit of confirmed melancholy. Besides, his constitution was never strong. Consumption seemed to be a hereditary disease of the family ; his father, sister, and three brothers having died of it. He, himself, often suffered from a pain in the chest, and he seems to have made up his mind therefore, that he too would die of this disease. His countenance assumed a pale and emaciated look ; nevertheless he worked hard at the correction of his first edition, and also continued to add fresh compositions. While in this melancholy state, the refusal of Mr. Constable—whose hands were already too full—to undertake the publication of his Second Edition, greatly added to the depression of his spirits, and he resolved to destroy everything which he had written. Thus, a hundred of his songs, most of which had never been printed, he burned, besides all those in which he had been engaged correcting for a re-issue ; and so bent was he on his work of destruction, that he requested his friends and acquaintances, to whom he had lent or given pieces, to return the manuscripts, so that nothing might be left after his death. Among those who visited him at this time was the Ettrick Shepherd. After a night spent in delightful congeniality of sentiment, Tannahill convoyed Mr Hogg as far as the "Half-Way" house between Glasgow and Paisley. When they parted, Tannahill mournfully exclaimed with tears in his eyes, "Farewell, we shall never meet again," a presentiment which was but too truly verified.

The day previous to his death he went to Glasgow, but his eyes then were wild and disordered, his pulse beat with violent agitation, and he complained of the treachery of his friends, the decay of his frame, and the unsupportable misery of his life. Such unequivocal proofs of mental derangement did he display that one of his friends considered it necessary to accompany him home to Paisley. His brothers hearing of his state hurried to his mother's house, and finding him already gone to bed, and apparently asleep, they left him thinking that next day he would be much better. One of the brothers, however, returned in about an hour after, and was greatly alarmed to find the door open and his brother gone. A search was immediately made, and in the dusk of the morning the coat of the poet

was found lying by the side of the Maxwelton Burn where
the Glasgow, Paisley, and Johnstone Canal crosses, by an
aqueduct, the little stream.   Peter Burnet* dived into the
pool and, to the intense grief of all, brought up the lifeless
body of Tannahill.   Thus died, 17th May, 1810, the poet
in his thirty-sixth year.

While we hurry over his melancholy end, we cannot but
heave a sigh that such a gifted life should set in so dark a
cloud.   Rather would we muse on the wonderful compositions of this Scottish son of toil, who has taught us many
lessons of purest morality, who has left a name as a song
writer little short of his great contemporary Burns, and
whose memory will never be forgotten so long as Scotland's
rugged mountains tower to the sky.

    *   *   *   *   *

One hundred years have now nearly come and gone since
Tannahill first saw the light in " Seestu."   Many gala days
during the cycle have been held in the quaint old town ;
but the Centenary of the poet's birth—the 3rd June, 1874
—promises to outstrip them all.   A holiday has been pro-
claimed—the Freemasons and the various Trades have made
arrangements for a procession, which is to end in a pic-nic
at " Tannahill's Well" on the " Braes"—houses and streets
are to be decorated—in the afternoon a Banquet is to be
held in the Abercorn Rooms, presided over by Provost
MURRAY, Chairman of the Tannahill Club ; and in the
evening a Concert, chiefly of Tannahill's Songs, is to take
place in the Drill Hall, at which THOMAS COATS, Esq., of
Ferguslie, will be Chairman ; and it is hoped that one result
of all this may be an enduring monument worthy of the
Poet, and worthy of the town which gave him birth.

The portrait of our author annexed to this volume is said
to be one of the best.   Of course an oil painting was beyond his reach or thought, and photography was not
then discovered.   There was no portrait of him taken
during his life, but after his death a sketch of his features
was taken, and it is from this that all the portraits have
emanated.

* Peter Burnet, or *Black Peter* as he was called in the district, was an
American Negro, and an acquaintance of one of Tannahill's brothers. The
relations of the poet ever afterwards showed him many attentions.

NOTES ON SONGS AND POEMS,

"Jessie, the Flower of Dumblane," is one of the most popular of Scottish Songs. He who wrote it was an observer of nature. The Music is by the poet's friend, Mr. R. A. Smith, and is worthy of the Song. Jessie is now believed to have been an imaginary fair one.

"The Lass o' Arranteenie."—This song was written upon a young woman whom a friend of Tannahill's met at Arranteenie, or Ardentinny, a beautiful spot on Loch Long, well known to Glasgow and West Country people. Some of the lines remind us of

"Full many a gem of purest ray serene,
The dark unfathomed caves of ocean bear ;
Full many a flower is born to blush unseen
And waste its sweetness in the desert air."

—The Music is by Mr Ross, of Aberdeen.

"The Braes o' Gleniffer" contains some splendid touches of nature, and is certainly among Tannahill's best. It is not, however, so well known as it deserves to be. The Braes were a great haunt of Tannahill. Within two miles of Paisley, and containing as they do a variety of beautiful scenery, they are much resorted to by lovers of nature from Paisley and the West of Scotland generally. From the summit of the Braes you have a most extensive prospect, and Mr Fulton, the proprietor at Glenfield, is most willing to allow all decent people to enter his part of them. The ruins of Stanley Castle—the "Auld Castle"—lies at the base of the hills, and is now surrounded by the water of Stanley Dam.

"Och, Hey, Johnnie Lad."—The scene of this trysting place is at the south side of the "Newton Woods." It is a very romantic spot. Formerly there stood here a small house with garden attached, called the Screechhill, which was given by the Laird, Mr Spiers, to one of his old servants named Caldwell, along with a portion of ground to graze a cow, as long as he lived. Along the Newton Woods was a favourite walk of the Poet's—and many a fine evening found him seated on the beer or old malt stone at the side of old Caldwell's door with his note book in hand—whence he could see every spot mentioned in the song—"Newton Woods," the "Firs sae green," "Whinny Knowe"—and at no other place around Paisley could whins be seen blooming in such perfection. The "Spunkie Howe" was a piece of ground not fit to be cultivated. It was while sitting on the stone at Caldwell's door that Tannahill wrote this truly humourous song. He gave it to Mrs Caldwell. The subjects of it were her daughter Janet and

her lad, John Stewart, whom, doubtless, the Poet had often met in
his walks in the district, and whose case it suited so well. Janet
Caldwell and Stewart were afterwards married, and lived in
Screechhill for sixty years. Only a few years since, after Mrs.
Stewart died, was the farmer allowed to take off the roof.

"POOR TOM, FARE-THEE-WELL."—In these lines the Poet
denounces in withering terms, the neglect, in old age, by the purse-
proud, of those who have spent their strength in their country's
service.

"RAB RORYSON'S BONNET."—Most of the persons described by
Tannahill were real, and it is believed that the model of this witty
and humorous song was either M'Neil, of Barra, or Riddell, of
Lochwinnoch.

"LASSIE TAK THE LAD YE LIKE."—No doubt the Poet had
some of his Paisley acquaintances in view in penning these lines.
Instances could not but be common, then as now, of a couple com-
mencing housekeeping in a small way, and, by industry and
economy, attaining to comfort and even affluence. This song and
his "Irish Farmer" prove that "True happiness has no localities."

"OH! ARE YE SLEEPING MAGGIE."—This is deservedly a
popular song—music being well fitted to the words. A wild
winter's night is most truthfully pictured out. Maggie is believed
to have been a cousin of the Poet's who lived near Beith.

"WALLACE'S LAMENT."—This song tries to describe the feelings
of the great hero after his terrible defeat by the English at Falkirk.
Though certainly far short of Burns' lines, we think they have been
much underrated. Elderslie, the birthplace of Wallace, is about
two miles west of Paisley. In Paisley Fountain Gardens may be
seen a young tree grown from an acorn of Wallace's tree which
grew at Elderslie.

"ACCUSE ME NOT."—It is believed that the Poet was in love
with some young woman, and that she proved false. Hence this
song.

"THE DUSKY GLEN."—The Glen here described was either the
Altpatrick Burn, near Elderslie, or the burn at Glenfield, near
which is the well called "Tannahill's Well."

"THROUGH CRUIKSTON CASTLE'S LONELY WA'S."—This old
Castle stands on a commanding eminence about midway between
Glasgow and Paisley, near the banks of the Canal. Queen Mary
of Scotland here awaited the issue of the battle of Langside.
Fortunately this old castle has found a preserver in its proprietor,
Sir John Maxwell. It is a favourite spot for pic-nic parties from
Glasgow and Paisley.

"GLOOMY WINTER'S NOO AWA."—This song for a considerable time enjoyed great popularity. It then became comparatively forgotten until the splendid singing of it by Miss E. Paton brought it once again into favour, and it has continued ever since to be a favourite. All the places named and described in it are within easy range of "Seestu."

"FROM HILL TO HILL" was written on the threatened invasion by Napoleon, and is really a very good warlike song—a class of which we are not particularly well possessed. Take away the Jacobite songs, and we have few of real merit.

"THOU BONNIE WOOD O' CRAIGIELEE."—Just outside Paisley, and near the present Gas Work was the wood. Not a vestige of it now remains to show us the spot where Tannahill and his young friends, the "West End Callans," went a bird nesting. While, however, the wood has gone, the song lives, and WILL as long as a true heart beats in a Scottish breast. It appeals not, however, to country—but, like all true poetry, to humanity.

"LOWLAN' LASSIE WILT THOU GO," is a truly good song, and deserves to be more widely known. The music was arranged by Mr Ross.

"THE COGGIE" is a good convivial song, and may be favourably compared with some of Burns' of the same class.

"COME HAME TO YOUR LINGELS."—Tannahill here describes scenes which unfortunately were too common then as now, and all caused by "Mununday's Yill."

"THE SOLDIER'S RETURN."—It may at once be admitted that this play has not been a success, though the careful reader will find in it many lines of high merit. The scene is laid at Altpatrick Burn, and the *Dramatis Personæ* were people known at the time. It was written at the request of the Poet's friend, Mr Archibald Pollock, comedian, who died just as it was commenced, and thus Tannahill lost the assistance of him who could have been of great use in his new and untried field.

"OH! DEATH, IT'S NO THY DEEDS I MOURN," was written on Alexander Wilson emigrating to America. Wilson was born in the Seedhill of Paisley, and like his contemporary, Tannahill, was brought up to the weaving trade. While at the loom, like Tannahill, he took to writing verse, but, unfortunately, in one of his pieces, he assaulted the private character of one of the Manufacturers. In legal proceedings which were taken against him, he found himself much humiliated, and this, together with discontentment at his lot, induced him to emigrate to America. Some of his pieces are of uncommon merit, but the best known of all is, perhaps, "Watty and Meg." For a description of character in that sphere it is unsurpassed. Alexander Wilson's great work, however, is his

"American Ornithology." He died at Philadelphia, 1813. A very fine statue of him in bronze and mounted on a pedestal was set up within the Paisley Abbey gates in 1874.

"THE NEGRO GIRL" is a very pathetic piece, picturing out very feelingly the miseries slavery inflicted on the Negro.

"THE WANDERING BARD."—The Poet here describes the reception which a wandering minstrel got at an inn. At that time Rhymers used to travel the country and repeat their pieces.

"THE FLOWER O' LEVERN SIDE."—The Levern is a tributary of the Cart, joining it near Cruikston Castle. "The Sunny Braes that skirt the Clyde" mentioned in this piece refer to the Kilpatrick Hills, which Tannahill could see from Gleniffer Braes

"THE DIRGE OF CAROLAN."—Carolan was the last of the Irish bards, and the most famous of them all. He died poor. Nearly every country has had its bards, and those acquainted with history will remember that the charge of murdering the Welsh bards, lest they should keep alive the independent spirit among the people, is brought against Edward I. Scotland had hers too—such as Blind Harry. France had her Troubadours, &c.

"THE KEBBUCKSTON WEDDING," is a very happy effusion, and pictures out the customs prevalent at marriages in Scotland at that time. Watty, the hero, was nobody knows who, but Willie Galbraith was a well known fiddler in Kilbarchan, who did good service at all surrounding convivial parties.

"THE TRIFLER'S SABBATH DAY" is a capital picture, and true to the life, of many who desecrate the Sabbath.

"THE PORTRAIT OF GUILT," is in imitation of Mr. Lewis, a romance writer, who was contemporary with Tannahill. The picture is a dreadful one.

"THE EPISTLE TO ALEXANDER BORLAND."—It was Mr. Borland whom Tannahill was visiting in Glasgow when it was noticed that his mind was deranged. Mr Borland accompanied him home.

"TOWSER—A TALE," was written on the death of the Poet's dog, which used to accompany him in all his rambles on Gleniffer Braes, in Newton Woods, by Cruikston Castle, &c.

TANNAHILL'S SONGS.

Jessie, the Flower o' Dumblane.

Music by R. A. Smith.

The sun has gane down o'er the lof-ty Ben-lo-mond, And

left the red clouds to pre-side o'er the scene; While lane-ly I

stray in the calm sim-mer gloam-in', To muse on sweet Jes-sie' the

flow'r o' Dum-blane. How sweet is the brier, wi' its saft fauld-ing

blos-som, And sweet is the birk, wi' its man-tle o' green; Yet

sweet-er an' fair-er, an' dear to this bo-som, Is love-ly young

Espress.

Jes-sie, the flow'r o' Dum-blane. Is love-ly young Jes-sie, Is

Tempo.

love-ly young Jes-sie, Is love-ly young Jes-sie, the flow'r o' Dumblane.

She's modest as ony, and blythe as she's bonnie,
  For guileless simplicity marks her its ain;
And far be the villain, divested o' feeling,
  Wha'd blight in its bloom the sweet flow'r o' Dumblane.
Sing on, thou sweet mavis, thy hymn to the e'ening,
  Thou'rt dear to the echoes of Calderwood glen;
Sae dear to this bosom, sae artless and winning,
  Is charming young Jessie, the flow'r o' Dumblane.

How lost were my days till I met wi' my Jessie,
  The sports o' the city seemed foolish and vain,
I ne'er saw a nymph I could ca' my dear lassie,
  Till charmed wi' sweet Jessie, the flow'r o' Dumblane.
Though mine were the station o' loftiest grandeur,
  Amidst its profusion I'd languish in pain;
And reckon as naething the height o' its splendour,
  If wanting sweet Jessie, the flow'r o' Dumblane.

While the Gray-Pinioned Lark.

WHILE the gray-pinioned lark early mounts to the skies,
  And cheerily hails the sweet dawn,
And the sun, newly risen, sheds the mist from his eyes,
  And smiles over mountain and lawn,
Delighted I stray by the fairy-wood side,
  Where the dewdrops the crowflowers adorn,
And nature arrayed in her midsummer's pride,
  Sweetly smiles to the smile of the morn.

Ye dark waving plantings, ye green shady bowers,
  Your charms ever varying I view;
My soul's dearest transports, my happiest hours,
  Have owed half their pleasures to you.
Sweet Ferguslie, hail! thou'rt the dear sacred grove,
  Where first my young muse spread her wing;
Here nature first waked me to rapture and love,
  And taught me her beauties to sing.

Loudon's Bonnie Woods and Braes.

Air—"Earl Moira's strathspey."

[The hero and heroine of this song were the Earl and Countess of Moira, afterwards Marquis and Marchioness of Hastings.]

LOUDON'S bonnie woods and braes,
  I maun lea' them a' lassie ;
Wha can thole when Britain's faes
  Would gie Britons law, lassie ?
Wha would shun the field o' danger ?
Wha frae fame wad live a stranger ?
Now when freedom bids avenge her,
  Wha would shun her ca' lassie ?
Loudon's bonnie woods and braes
Ha'e seen our happy bridal days,
And gentle hope shall soothe thy waes,
  When I am far awa', lassie.

Hark ! the swelling bugle sings,
  Yielding joy to thee, laddie ;
But the doleful bugle brings
  Waefu' thoughts to me, laddie.
Lonely I maun climb the mountain,
Lonely stray beside the fountain,
Still the weary moments countin',
  Far frae love and thee, laddie.
O'er the gory fields o' war,
When vengeance drives his crimson car,
Thou'lt maybe fa', frae me afar,
  And nane to close thy e'e, laddie.

Oh, resume thy wonted smile !
  Oh, suppress thy fears, lassie !
Glorious honour crowns the toil
  That the soldier shares, lassie.
Heaven will shield thy faithful lover,
Till the vengeful strife is over,
Then we'll meet, nae mair to sever,
  Till the day we die, lassie ;

'Midst our bonnie woods and braes,
We'll spend our peaceful, happy days,
As blythe's yon lightsome lamb that plays
  On Loudon's flowery lea, lassie.

The Lass o' Arranteenie.

Air—"The lass o' Arranteenie."

FAR lone, amang the Highland hills,
  'Midst nature's wildest grandeur,
By rocky dens and woody glens,
  With weary steps I wander :
The langsome way, the darksome day,
  The mountain mist sae rainy,
Are nought to me when gaun to thee,
  Sweet lass o' Arranteenie.

Yon mossy rosebud down the howe,
  Just opening fresh and bonnie,
Blinks sweetly 'neath the hazel bough,
  And's scarcely seen by ony :
Sae sweet amid her native hills,
  Obscurely blooms my Jeanie ;
Mair fair and gay than rosy May,
  The flower o' Arranteenie.

Now, from the mountain's lofty brow,
  I view the distant ocean ;
There avarice guides the bounding prow,
  Ambition courts promotion.
Let fortune pour her golden store,
  Her laurelled favours many ;
Give me but this, my soul's first wish,
  The lass o' Arranteenie.

The Braes o' Gleniffer.

Air—" Saw ye my wee thing."

KEEN blaws the wind o'er the braes o' Gleniffer,
  The auld castle's turrets are covered wi' snaw ;
How changed frae the time when I met wi' my lover
  Amang the broom bushes by Stanley green shaw ;

The wild flowers o' simmer were spread a' sae bonnie,
    The mavis sung sweet frae the green birken tree ;
But far to the camp they ha'e marched my dear Johnnie,
    And now it is winter wi' nature and me.

Then ilk thing around us was blythesome and cheerie,
    Then ilk thing around us was bonnie and braw ;
Now naething is heard but the wind whistling dreary,
    And naething is seen but the wide-spreading snaw.
The trees are a' bare, and the birds mute and dowie ;
    They shake the cauld drift frae their wings as they flee,
And chirp out their plaints, seeming wae for my Johnnie ;
    'Tis winter wi' them and 'tis winter wi' me.

Yon cauld sleety cloud skiffs alang the bleak mountain,
    And shakes the dark firs on the steep rocky brae,
While down the deep glen bawls the snaw-flooded fountain,
    That murmured sae sweet to my laddie and me.
'Tis no its loud roar on the wint'ry wind swellin',
    'Tis no the cauld blast brings the tear i' my e'e,
For, oh, gin I saw but my bonnie Scots callan,
    The dark days o' winter were simmer to me !

Johnnie, Lad.

Air—"The lasses of the ferry."

Och, hey ! Johnnie, lad,
    Ye're no sae kind's ye should ha'e been ;
Och, hey ! Johnnie, lad,
    Ye didna keep your tryst yestreen :
I waited lang beside the wood,
    Sae wae and weary, a' my lane ;
Och, hey ! Johnnie, lad,
    Ye're no sae kind's ye should ha'e been.

I looked by the whinny knowe,
    I looked by the firs sae green,
I looked o'er the spunkie howe,
    And aye I thought you would ha'e been.
The ne'er a supper crossed my craig,
    The ne'er a sleep has closed my e'en ;
Och, hey ! Johnnie, lad,
    Ye're no sae kind's ye should ha'e been.

Gin ye were waiting by the wood,
  Then I was waiting by the thorn,
I thought it was the place we set,
And waited maist till dawning morn.
Sae be na vexed, my bonnie lassie,
  Let my waiting stand for thine,
We'll awa' to Craigton shaw,
  And seek the joys we tint yestreen.

The Braes of Balquhither.

Air—"The three carles o' Buchanan."

LET us go, lassie, go
  To the braes of Balquhither,
Where the blaeberries grow
  'Mang the bonnie Highland heather;
Where the deer and the rae,
  Lightly bounding together,
Sport the lang simmer day
  On the braes o' Balquhither.

I will twine thee a bower,
  By the clear siller fountain,
And I'll cover it o'er
  Wi' the flowers o' the mountain.
I will range through the wilds,
  And the deep glens sae dreary,
And return wi' their spoils,
  To the bower o' my dearie.

When the rude wintry win'
  Idly raves round our dwelling,
And the roar of the linn
  On the night breeze is swelling;
So merrily we will sing,
  As the storm rattles o'er us,
'Till the dear sheeling ring
  Wi' the light lilting chorus.

Now the simmer is in prime,
  Wi' the flowers richly blooming,
And the wild mountain thyme
  A' the moorlands perfuming ;
To our dear native scenes ·
  Let us journey together,
Where glad innocence reigns,
  'Mang the braes o' Balquhither.

Fly we to some Desert Isle.

FLY we to some desert isle,
  There we'll pass our days together,
Shun the world's derisive smile,
  Wandering tenants of the heather ;
Sheltered in some lowly glen,
Far removed from mortal ken,
Forget the selfish ways o' men,
  Nor feel a wish beyond each other.

Though my friends deride me still,
  Jamie I'll disown thee never ;
Let them scorn me as they will,
  I'll be thine, and thine for ever.
What are a' my kin' to me,
A' their pride of pedigree ?
What were life, if wanting thee,
  And what were death if we maun sever ?

Oh, sair I rue the witless wish.

OH, sair I rue the witless wish,
  That gar'd me gang wi' you at e'en ;
And sair I rue the birken bush,
  That screened us wi' its leaves sae green :
And though you vowed you would be mine,
  The tear o' grief aye dims my e'e ;
For, oh ! I'm feared that I may tine
  The love that you ha'e promised me !

While ithers seek their e'ening sports,
   I wander dowie, a' my lane,
For when I join my glad resorts,
   Their dalling gi'es me meikle pain.
Alas, it was na sae short syne,
   When a' my nights were spent wi' glee;
But, oh! I'm feared that I may tine
   The love that you ha'e promised me.

Dear lassie, keep thy heart aboon,
   For I ha'e waired my winter's fee :
I've coft a bonnie silken gown,
   To be a bridal gift for thee.
And sooner shall the hill fa' down,
   And mountain high shall stand the sea,
Ere I'd accept a gouden crown,
   To change that love I bear for thee.

***

Kitty Tyrell.

THE breeze of the night fans the dark mountain's breast,
And the light bounding deer have all sunk to their rest;
The big sullen waves lash the loch's rocky shore,
And the lone drowsy fisherman nods on his oar.
Though pathless the moor, and though starless the skies,
The star of my heart is my Kitty's bright eyes;
And joyful I hie over glen, brake, and fell,
In secret to meet my sweet Kitty Tyrell.

Ah! long we have loved in her father's despite,
And oft we have met at the dead hour of night,
When hard-hearted vigilance, sunk in repose,
Gave love one sweet hour its fond tale to disclose.
These moments of transport, to me, oh, how dear!
And the fate that would part us, alas, how severe!
Although the rude storm rise with merciless swell,
This night I shall meet my sweet Kitty Tyrell.

Ah! turn, hapless youth! see the dark cloud of death,
Comes rolling in gloom o'er the wild haunted heath;
Deep groans the scathed oak on the glen's cliffy brow,
And the sound of the torrent seems heavy with woe.

Away, foolish seer, with thy fancies so wild,
Go, tell thy weak dreams to some credulous child;
Love guides my light steps through the lone dreary dell,
And I fly to the arms of sweet Kitty Tyrell.

Mine ain Dear Somebody.

Air—" Were I obliged to beg."

WHEN gloaming treads the heels of day,
And birds sit cowering on the spray,
Alang the flowery hedge I stray,
    To meet mine ain dear somebody.

The scented brier, the fragrant bean,
The clover bloom, the dewy green,
A' charm me as 1 rove at e'en,
    To meet mine ain dear somebody.

Let warriors prize the hero's name,
Let mad ambition tower for fame,
I'm happier in my lowly hame,
    Obscurely bless'd wi' somebody.

Despairing Mary.

MARY, why thus waste thy youthtime in sorrow?
    See a' around you the flowers sweetly blaw;
Blythe sets the sun o'er the wild cliffs of Jura,
    Blythe sings the mavis in ilka green shaw!
How can this heart ever mair think of pleasure,
    Simmer may smile, but delight I ha'e nane;
Cauld in the grave lies my heart's only treasure,
    Nature seems dead since my Jamie is gane.

This kerchief he gave me, a true lover's token,
    Dear, dear to me was the gift for his sake!
I wear't near my heart, but this poor heart is broken,
    Hope died with Jamie, and left it to break.
Sighing for him I lie down in the e'ening,
    Sighing for him I awake in the morn;
Spent are my days a' in secret repining,
    Peace to this bosom can never return.

Oft have we wandered in sweetest retirement,
　　Telling our loves 'neath the moon's silent beam ;
Sweet were our meetings of tender endearment.
　　But fled are these joys like a fleet passing dream.
Cruel remembrance, ah ! why wilt thou rack me ?
　　Brooding o'er joys that for ever are flown ;
Cruel remembrance, in pity forsake me,
　　Flee to some bosom where grief is unknown !

Poor Tom, Fare-thee-well.

'Mongst life's many cares there is none so provoking,
　　As when a brave seaman, disabled and old,
Must crouch to the worthless, and stand the rude mocking
　　Of those who have nought they can boast but their gold :
Poor Tom, once so high on the list of deserving,
　　By captain and crew none so dearly were prized,
At home now laid up, worn with many years' serving,
　　Poor Tom takes his sup, and poor Tom is despised.

Yet, care thrown a-lee, see old Tom in his glory,
　　Placed snug with a shipmate, whose life once he saved,
Recounting the feats of some bold naval story,
　　The battles they fought, and the storms they had braved.
In his country's defence he has dared every danger,
　　His valorous deeds he might boast undisguised ;
Yet home-hearted landsmen hold Tom as a stranger,
　　Poor Tom loves his sup, and poor Tom is depised.

Myself, too, am old, rather rusted for duty,
　　Yet still I'll prefer the wide ocean to roam ;
I'd join some bold corsair, and live upon booty,
　　Before I'd be gibed by these sucklings at home.
Poor Tom, fare-thee-well ! for, by heaven, 'tis provoking,
　　When thus a brave seaman, disabled and old,
Must crouch to the worthless, and stand the rude mocking.
　　Of those who have nought they can boast but their gold.

Barrochan Jean.
Air—"Johnnie M'Gill."

'Tis ha'ena ye heard, man, o' Barrochan Jean ?
　　And ha'ena ye heard, man, o' Barrochan Jean ?

How death and starvation cam' o'er the whole nation,
    She wrought sic mischief wi' her twa pawky een.
The lads and the lasses were dying in dizzens,
    The ane killed with love, and the tither wi' spleen ;
The ploughing, the sawing, the shearing, the mawing,
    A' wark was forgotten for Barrochan Jean.

Frae the south and the north, o'er the Tweed and the Forth,
    Sic coming and ganging there never was seen ;
The comers were cheerie, the gangers were blearie,
    Despairing or hoping for Barrochan Jean.
The carlins at hame were a' girning and graning,
    The bairns were a' greeting frae morning till e'en ;
They get naething for crowdy but runts boiled to sowdy,
    For naething got growing for Barrochan Jean.

The doctors declared it was past their describing,
    The ministers said 'twas a judgment for sin ;
But they looked sae blae, and their hearts were sae wae,
    I was sure they were dying for Barrochan Jean.
The burns on road-sides were a' dry wi' their drinking,
    Yet a' wadna sloken the drouth i' their skin ;
A' round the peat-stacks, and alangst the dyke backs,
    E'en the winds were a' sighing, sweet Barrochan Jean !

The timmer ran done wi' making o' coffins,
    Kirkyards o' their sward were a' howkit fu' clean ;
Dead lovers were packed like herring in barrels,
    Sic thousands were dying for Barrochan Jean.
But mony braw thanks to the laird o' Glenbrodie,
    The grass owre their graves is now bonnie and green ;
He stole the proud heart o' our wanton young lady,
    And spoiled a' the harms o' her twa pawky een.

Rab Roryson's Bonnet.

Air—"The auld wife o' the glen."

YE'LL a' hae heard tell o' Rab Roryson's bonnet,
Ye'll a' hae heard tell o' Rab Roryson's bonnet ;
'Twas no for itsel', 'twas the head that was in it,
Gar'd a' bodies talk o' Rab Roryson's bonnet.

This bonnet, that theekit his wonderfu' head,
Was his shelter in winter, in simmer his shade;
And at kirk, or at market, or bridals, I ween,
A braw gawcier bonnet there never was seen.

Wi' a round rosy tap, like a meikle blackboyd,
It was slouched just a kenning on ither hand side;
Some maintained it was black, some maintained it was blue,
It had something o' baith, as a body may trow.

But, in sooth, I assure you, for ought that I saw,
Still his bonnet had naething uncommon ava';
Though the whole parish talked o' Rab Roryson's bonnet,
'Twas a' for the marvellous head that was in it.

That head, let it rest, it is now in the mools,
Though in life a' the warld beside it were fools;
Yet o' what kind o' wisdom his head was possessed,
Nane e'er kenned but himsel', sae there's nane that will
    miss't.

———

When John and me were married.

Air—"Clean pease strae."

WHEN John and me were married,
    Our hadding was but sma',
For my minnie, cankered carling,
    Would gi'e us nought ava':
I wair't my fee wi' cannie care,
    As far as it would gae,
But weel I wat our bridal bed
    Was clean pease strae.

Wi' working late and early,
    We're come to what you see;
For fortune thrave aneath our hand,
    Sae eydent aye were we.
The lowe o' love made labour light,
    I'm sure ye'll find it sae,
When kind ye cuddle down at e'en,
    'Mang clean pease strae.

The rose blooms gay on cairney brae,
 As weel's in birken shaw,
And love will lowe in cottage low,
 As weel's in lofty ha';
Sae, lassie, tak' the lad ye like,
 Whate'er your minnie say,
Though you should mak' your bridal bed
 O' clean pease strae.

The Irish Farmer.

Air—"Sir John Scott's favourite."

DEAR Judy, when first we got married,
 Our fortune indeed was but small,
For save the light hearts that we carried,
 Our riches were nothing at all:
I sung while I reared up the cabin,
 Ye powers give me vigour and health,
And a truce to all sighing and sobbing,
 For love is Pat Mulligan's wealth.

Through summer and winter so dreary,
 I cheerily toiled on the farm,
Nor ever once dreamed growing weary,
 For love gave my labour its charm.
And now, though 'tis weak to be vaunty,
 Yet here let us gratefully own,
We live amidst pleasure and plenty,
 As happy's the king on the throne.

We've Murdoch, and Patrick, and Connor,
 As fine little lads as you'll see,
And Kitty, sweet girl, 'pon my honour,
 She's just the dear picture of thee.
Though some folks may still underrate us,
 Ah, why should we mind them a fig?
We've a large swinging field of potatoes,
 A good driminduath* and a pig.

* Driminduath is a general name in Ireland for the cow.

Dear Judy.

DEAR JUDY, I've taken a-thinking,
　　The children their letters must learn,
And we'll send for old Father O'Jenking,
　　To teach them three months in the barn:
For learning's the way to promotion,
　　'Tis culture brings fruit from the sod,
And books give a fellow a notion
　　How matters are doing abroad.

Though father neglected my reading,
　　Kind soul, sure his spirit's in rest!
For the very first part of his breeding,
　　Was still to relieve the distressed.
And, late, when the traveller benighted,
　　Besought hospitality's claim,
He lodged him till morning, delighted,
　　Because 'twas a lesson to them.

The man that wont feel for another,
　　Is just like a colt on the moor,
He lives without knowing a brother,
　　To frighten bad luck from his door.
But he that's kind-hearted and steady,
　　Though wintry misfortune should come,
He'll still find some friend who is ready
　　To scare the old witch from his home.

Success to old Ireland for ever!
　　'Tis just the dear land to my mind,
Her lads are warm-hearted and clever,
　　Her girls are all handsome and kind.
And he that her name would bespatter,
　　By wishing the French safely o'er,
May the de'il blow him over the water,
　　And make him cook frogs for the core.

The Highlander's Invitation.
Air—"Will ye come to the bower?"

WILL you come to the board I've prepared for you?
Your drink shall be good, of the true Highland blue;

Will you, Donald, will you, Callum, come to the board?
There each shall be great as her own native lord.

There'll be plenty of pipe, and a glorious supply
Of the good sneesh-tc bacht, and the fine cut-and-dry:
Will you, Donald, will you, Callum, come then at e'en?
There be some for the stranger, but more for the frien'.

There we'll drink foggy care to his gloomy abodes,
And we'll smoke till we sit in the clouds like the gods:
Will you, Donald, will you, Callum, wont you do so?
'Tis the way that our forefathers did long ago.

And we'll drink to the Cameron, we'll drink to Lochiel,
And, for Charlie, we'll drink all the French to the de'il:
Will you, Donald, will you, Callum, drink there until
There be heads lie like peats if hersel' had her will.

There be groats on the land, there be fish in the sea,
And there's fouth in the coggie for friendship and me:
Come then, Donald, come then, Callum, come then to-night,
Sure the Highlander be first in the fuddle and the fight.

Oh, are ye Sleeping, Maggie?

Air—"Sleepy Maggie."

Oh, are ye sleeping, Maggie?
Oh, are ye sleeping, Maggie?
Let me in, for loud the linn
Is roaring o'er the warlock craigie.

Mirk and rainy is the night,
    No a starn in a' the carry,
Lightnings gleam athwart the lift,
    And winds drive wi' winter's fury.
        Oh, are ye sleeping, Maggie? &c.

Fearful soughs the boortree bank,
    The rifted wood roars wild and dreary,
Loud the iron yett does clank,
    And cry of howlets mak's me eerie.
        Oh, are ye sleeping, Maggie? &c.

Aboon my breath I daurna speak,
  For fear I rouse your waukrife daddie,
Caulds the blast upon my cheek,
  Oh, rise, rise, my bonny lady.
       Oh, are ye sleeping, Maggie? &c.

She oped the door, she let him in,
  He cuist aside his dreeping plaidie:
"Blaw your warst, ye rain and win',
  Since, Maggie, now I'm in aside ye."

  Now since ye're waking, Maggie,
  Now since ye're waking, Maggie,
  What care I for howlet's cry,
  For boortree bank, or warlock craigie.

The Lament of Wallace after the Battle of Falkirk.

Air—"Maids of Arrochar."

Thou dark-winding Carron, once pleasing to see,
  To me thou canst never give pleasure again;
My brave Caledonians lie low on the lea,
  And thy streams are deep-tinged with the blood of the
    slain.

Ah! base-hearted treachery has doomed our undoing,
  My poor bleeding country, what more can I do?
Even valour looks pale o'er the red field of ruin,
  And freedom beholds her best warriors laid low.

Farewell, ye dear partners of peril! farewell!
  Though buried ye lie in one wide bloody grave,
Your deeds shall ennoble the place where you fell,
  And your names be enrolled with the sons of the brave.

But I, a poor outcast, in exile must wander,
  Perhaps like a traitor ignobly must die!
On thy wrongs, oh, my country! indignant I ponder;
  Ah! woe to the hour when thy Wallace must fly.

The Worn Soldier.

THE Queensferry boatie rows light,
   And light is the heart that it bears,
For it brings the poor soldier safe back to his home,
   From many long toilsome years.

How sweet are his green native hills,
   As they smile to the beams of the west,
But sweeter by far is the sunshine of hope
   That gladdens the soldier's breast.

I can well mark the tears of his joy,
   As the wave-beaten pier he ascends,
For already, in fancy, he enters his home,
   'Midst the greetings of tender friends.

But fled are his visions of bliss,
   All his transports but rose to deceive,
He found the dear cottage a tenantless waste,
   And his kindred all sunk in the grave.

Lend a sigh to the soldier's grief,
   For now he is helpless and poor,
And forced to solicit a slender relief,
   He wanders from door to door.

To him let our answers be mild,
   And, oh! to the sufferer be kind!
For the look of indifference, the frown of disdain,
   Bear hard on a generous mind.

The Farewell.

Air—"Lord Gregory."

ACCUSE me not, inconstant fair,
   Of being false to thee,
For I was true, would still been so,
   Hadst thou been true to me.

But when I knew thy plighted lips
   Once to a rival's pressed,
Love-smothered independence rose,
   And spurned thee from my breast.

The fairest flower in nature's field
   Conceals the rankling thorn ;
So thou, sweet flower ! as false as fair,
   This once kind heart hath torn.
'Twas mine to prove the fellest pangs
   That slighted love can feel ;
'Tis thine to weep that one rash act
   Which bids this long farewell.

Wi' waefu' Heart.

Air—"Sweet Annie frae the sea-beach came."

Wi' waefu' heart and sorrowing e'e
   I saw my Jamie sail awa',
Oh ! 'twas a fatal day to me,
   That day he passed the Berwick Law ;
How joyless now seemed all behind !
   I lingering strayed along the shore ;
Dark boding fears hung on my mind
   That I might never see him more.

The night came on with heavy rain,
   Loud, fierce, and wild the tempest blew ;
In mountains rolled the awful main :
   Ah, hapless maid ! my fears how true !
The landsmen heard their drowning cries,
   The wreck was seen with dawning day ;
My love was found, and now he lies
   Low in the isle of gloomy May.

O boatman, kindly waft me o'er !
   The caverned rock shall be my home ;
'Twill ease my burdened heart to pour
   Its sorrows o'er his grassy tomb ;
With sweetest flowers I'll deck his grave,
   And tend them through the langsome year ;
I'll water them, ilk morn and eve,
   With deepest sorrow's warmest tear.

The Kebbuckston Wedding.

Written to an ancient Highland Air.

AULD WATTY o' Kebbuckston brae,
  Wi' lear and reading o' books auld farren,
What think ye ! the body came owre the day,
  An tauld us he's gaun to be married to Mirren.
We a' got a bidding to gang to the wedding,
  Baith Johnnie and Sandie, and Nellie and Nannie ;
And Tam o' the Knowes, he swears and he vows,
  At the dancing he'll face to the bride wi' his grannie.

A' the lads ha'e trysted their joes ;
  Slee Willie cam' up and ca'd on Nelly ;
Although she was hecht to Geordie Bowse,
  She's gien him the gunk, and she's gaun wi' Willie.
Wee collier Johnnie has yoked his pony,
  An's aff to the town for a lading o' nappy ;
Wi' fouth o' good meat to serve us to eat,
  Sae wi' fuddling and feasting we'll a' be fu' happy.

Wee Patie Brydie's to say the grace,
  The body's aye ready at dredgies and weddings ;
And flunkie M'Fee, of the Skiverton place,
  Is chosen to scuttle the pies and the puddings.
For there'll be plenty o' ilka thing dainty,
  Baith lang kail and haggis, and everything fitting ;
Wi' luggies o' beer, our wizzens to clear,
  Sae the de'il fill his kyte wha gaes clung frae the meeting.

Lowrie has coft Gibbie Cameron's gun,
  That his auld gutcher bore when he followed Prince
    Charlie ;
The barrel was rusted as black as the grun',
  But he's ta'en't to the smiddy, an's fettled it rarely.
Wi' wallets o' pouther his musket he'll shouther,
  And ride at our head, to the bride's a-parading ;
At ilka farm toun he'll fire them three roun',
  Till the hale kintra ring wi' the Kebbuckston wedding.

Jamie and Johnnie maun ride the brouse,
   For few like these can sit in the saddle;
And Willie Cobreath, the best o' bows,
   Is trysted to jig in the barn wi' his fiddle.
Wi' whisking and flisking, and reeling and wheeling,
   The young anes are like to loup out o' the body,
And Neilie M'Nairn, though sair forfairn,
   He vows that he'll wallop twa sets wi' the howdie.

Sauney M'Nab, wi' his tartan trews,
   Has hecht to come down in the midst o' the caper,
And gi'e us three wallops o' merry shan trews,
   Wi' the true Highland fling o' Macrimmon the piper.
Sic hipping and skipping, and springing and flinging,
   I'se wad that there nane in the Lawlands can waft it!
Faith! Willie maun fiddle, and jirgum and diddle,
   And screed till the sweat fa' in beads frae his haffet.

Then gi'e me your hand, my trusty good frien',
   And gi'e me your word, my worthy auld kimmer,
Ye'll baith come owre on Friday bedeen,
   And join us in ranting and tooming the timmer.
With fouth o' good liquor, we'll haud at the bicker,
   And lang may the mailing o' Kebbuckston flourish;
For Watty's sae free, between you and me,
   I'se warrant he's bidden the half o' the parish.

The Five Friends.

Air—"We're a' noddin'."

WEEL, wha's in the bouroch, and what is your cheer?
The best that ye'll find in a thousand year.
          And we're a' noddin', nid nid noddin',
          We're a' noddin' fu' at e'en.

There's our ain Jamie Clark, frae the hall o' Argyle,
'Tis his leal Scottish heart, and his kind open smile.
          And we're a' noddin', &c.

There is Will the guid fallow, wha kills a' our care
Wi' his sang and his joke, and a mutchkin mair.
          And we're a' noddin', &c.

There is blythe Jamie Barr, frae St. Barchan's town,
When wit gets a kingdom he's sure o' the crown.
   And we're a' noddin', &c.

There is Rab, frae the south, wi' his fiddle and his flute;
I could list to his sangs till the starns fa' out.
   And we're a' noddin', &c.

Apollo, for our comfort, has furnished the Lowl,
And here is my bardship, as blind as an owl.
   For we're a noddin', &c.

Hey, Donald! How, Donald!

[The first verse and chorus by Tannahill, the other two verses by
William Motherwell.]

Though simmer smiles on bank and brae,
And nature bids the heart be gay,
Yet a' the joys o' flowery May
 Wi' pleasure ne'er can move me.
  Hey, Donald! how, Donald!
  Think upon your vow, Donald;
  Mind the heathery knowe, Donald,
  Where you vowed to love me.

The budding rose and scented brier,
The siller fountain skinkling clear,
The merry lav'rock whistling near,
 Wi' pleasure ne'er can move me.
  Hey, Donald! &c.

I downa look on bank and brae,
I downa greet whare a' are gay,
But oh! my heart will break wi' wae,
 Gin Donald cease to love me.
  Hey, Donald! &c.

Meg o' the Glen.

Air—"When she cam' ben she bobbit."

[The first two verses by Tannahill, the second two by Motherwell.]

Meg o' the glen set aff to the fair,
Wi' ruffles, and ribbons, and meikle prepare;
Her heart it was heavy, her head it was light,
For a' the lang way for a wooer she sighed.

She spak' to the lads, but the lads slipped by,
She spak' to the lasses, the lasses were shy;
She thought she might do, but she didna weel ken,
For nane seemed to care for poor Meg o' the glen.

"But wot ye, what was't made the lads a' gae by?
And wot ye, what was't made the lassies sae shy?
Poor Meg o' the glen had nae tocher ava,
And therefore could neither be bonnie nor braw:

"But an uncle wha lang in the Indies had been,
Foreseeing death coming to close his auld een,
Made his will, left her heiress o' thousand pounds ten,
Now, wha is mair thought o' than Meg o' the glen?"

The Lassie o' Merry Eighteen.

My father wad ha'e me to marry the miller,
    My mither wad ha'e me to marry the laird,
But brawly I ken it's the love o' the siller,
    That brightens their fancy to ony regard.
The miller is crooked, the miller is crabbed,
    The laird, though he's wealthy, he's lyart and lean;
He's auld, and he's cauld, and he's blin', and he's bald,
    And he's no for a lassie o' merry eighteen.

"But oh, there's a laddie wha tells me he lo'es me,
    And him I lo'e dearly, ay, dearly as life;
Though father and mither should scold and abuse me,
    Nae ither shall ever get me for a wife.
Although he can boast na o' land, nor yet siller,
    He's worthy to match wi' a duchess or queen;
For his heart is sae warm, and sae stately his form,
    And then, like mysel', he's just merry eighteen."

Oh, How can you gang, Lassie?

Air—"The bonniest lassie in a' the warld."

Oh, how can you gang, lassie, how can you gang,
    Oh how can you gang sae to grieve me?

Wi' your beauty and your art, ye hae broken my heart,
  For I never, never dreamed ye could leave me.
"Ah, wha wad ha'e thought that sae bonnie a face
  Could e'er wear a smile to deceive me?
Or that guile in that fair bosom could e'er find a place,
  And that you wad break your vow thus, and leave me?

"Oh, have you not mind when our names you entwined
  In a wreath round the purse you did weave me?
Or ha'e you now forgot the once dear trysting spot,
  Where so soft you pledged your faith ne'er to leave me?
But, changing as the wind is your light, fickle mind,
  Your smiles, tokens, vows, all deceive me;
No more, then, I'll trust to such frail painted dust,
  But bewail my fate till kind death relieve me.

"Then gang, fickle fair, to your new-fangled jo,
  Yes, gang, and in wretchedness leave me;
But alas! should you be doomed to a wedlock of woe,
  Ah, how would your unhappiness grieve me!
For, Mary! all faithless and false as thou art,
  Thy spell-binding glances, believe me,
So closely are entwined round this fond foolish heart,
  That the grave alone of them can bereave me."

The Lasses a' Leugh.

Air—"Kissed yestreen."

THE lasses a' leugh, and the carlin flate,
But Maggie was sitting fu' eerie and blate,
The auld silly gawkie, she couldna contain,
How brawly she was kissed yestreen;
  Kissed yestreen, kissed yestreen.
How brawly she was kissed yestreen:
She blethered it round to her fae and her frien',
How brawly she was kissed yestreen.

"She loosed the white napkin frae 'bout her dun neck,
And cried, The big sorrow tak' lang Geordie Fleck:
D'ye see what a scart I gat frae a preen,
By his towsling and kissing at me yestreen;

At me yestreen, at me yestreen,
By his towsling and kissing at me yestreen :
I canna conceive what the fellow could mean,
   By kissing sae meikle at me yestreen.

" Then she pu'd up her sleeve, and shawed a blae mark,
Quoth she, I gat that frae young Davy, our clerk ;
But the creature had surely forgat himsel' clean,
When he nipped me sae hard for a kiss yestreen ;
   For a kiss yestreen, for a kiss yestreen,
When he nipped me sae hard for a kiss yestreen :
I wonder what keepit my nails frae his een,
   When he nipped me sae hard for a kiss yestreen

" Then she held up her cheek, and cried, Foul fa' the laird,
Just look what I gat wi' his black birsie beard !
The vile filthy body ! was e'er the like seen ?
To rub me sae sair for a kiss yestreen ;
   For a kiss yestreen, for a kiss yestreen,
To rub me sae sair for a kiss yestreen ;
I'm sure that nae woman o' judgment need grien,
   To be rubbed, like me, for a kiss yestreen.

" Syne she tauld what grand offers she aften had had,
But wad she tak' a man ? na, she wasna sae mad :
For the whole o' the sex she cared no a preen,
And she hated the way she was kissed yestreen ;
   She was kissed yestreen, she was kissed yestreen,
And she hated the way she was kissed yestreen ;
'Twas a mercy that naething mair serious had been,
   For it's dangerous, whiles, to be kissed at e'en."

Our Bonnie Scots Lads.

Our bonnie Scots lads in their green tartan plaids,
   Their blue-belted bonnets, and feathers sae braw,
Ranked up on the green were fair to be seen,
   But my bonnie young laddie was fairest of a' ;
His cheeks were as red as the sweet heather-bell,
   Or the red western cloud looking down on the snaw ;
His lang yellow hair o'er his braid shoulders fell,
   And the een o' the lassies were fixed on him a'.

My heart sunk wi' wae on the wearifu' day,
   When torn frae my bosom they marched him awa',
He bade me farewell, he cried, "Oh, be leal!"
   And his red cheeks were wet wi' the tears that did fa'.
Ah! Harry, my love, though thou ne'er shouldst return,
   Till life's latest hour I thy absence will mourn;
And memory shall fade like a leaf on the tree,
   Ere my heart spare ae thought on anither but thee.

We'll meet beside the Dusky Glen.

WE'EL meet beside the dusky glen, on yon burn side,
Where the bushes form a cozie den, on yon burn side;
Though the broomy knowes be green, yet, there we may be
   seen,
But we'el meet, we'el meet at e'en down by yon burn side.

I'll lead thee to the birken bower, on yon burn side,
Sae sweetly wove wi' woodbine flower, on yon burn side;
There the busy prying eye ne'er disturbs the lover's joy,
While in ither's arms they lie, down by yon burn side.

Awa', ye rude unfeeling crew, frae yon burn side,
Those fairy scenes are no for you, by yon burn side;
There fancy smoothes her theme, by the sweetly murmuring
   stream,
And the rock-lodged echoes skim, down by yon burn side.

Now the planting taps are tinged wi' goud on yon burn side,
And gloamin' draws her foggy shroud o'er yon burn side;
Far frae the noisy scene, I'll through the fields alane,
There we'el meet, my ain dear Jean! down by yon burn side.

The Flower o' Levern Side.

YE sunny braes that skirt the Clyde,
   Wi' simmer flowers sae braw,
There's ae sweet flower on Levern side,
   That's fairer than them a':

Yet aye it droops its head in wae,
Regardless o' the sunny ray,
And wastes its sweets frae day to day,
    Beside the lonely shaw.

Wi' leaves a' steeped in sorrow's dew,
Fause, cruel man, it seems to rue:
Wha aft the sweeter power will pu',
    Then rend its heart in twa.
Thou bonnie flower on Levern side,
    Oh, gin thou'lt be but mine ;
I'll tend thee wi' a lover's pride,
    Wi' love that ne'er shall tine.

I'll tak' thee to my sheltering bower,
And shield thee frae the beating shower,
Unharmed by aught, thou't bloom secure
    Frae a' the blasts that blaw :
Thy charms surpass the crimson dye
That streaks the glowing western sky ;
But, here, unshaded, soon thou't die,
    And lone will be thy fa'.

Cruikston Castle's Lonely Wa's

THROUGH Cruikston Castle's lonely wa's
    The wintry wind howls wild and dreary ;
Though mirk the cheerless e'ening fa's,
    Yet I ha'e vowed to meet my Mary ;
Yes, Mary, though the wind should rave
    Wi' jealous spite to keep me frae thee,
The darkest stormy night I'd brave,
    For ae sweet secret moment wi' thee.

Loud o'er Cardonald's rocky steep,
    Rude Cartha pours in boundless measure ;
But I will ford the whirling deep,
    That roars between me and my treasure :
Yes, Mary, though the torrent rave
    Wi' jealous spite to keep me frae thee,
Its deepest flood I'd bauldly brave,
    For ae sweet secret moment wi' thee.

The watch-dog's howling loads the biast,
　And makes the nightly wanderer eerie,
But when the lonesome way is past,
　I'll to this bosom clasp my Mary.
Yes, Mary, though stern winter rave,
　Wi' a' his storms to keep me frae thee,
The wildest dreary night I'd brave,
　For ae sweet secret moment wi' thee.

I'll hie me to the Sheeling Hill.

Air—" Ghillie Callum."

I'LL hie me to the sheeling hill,
　And bide amang the braes, Callum ;
Ere I gang to Crochan mill,
　I'll live on hips and slaes, Callam.
Wealthy pride but ill can hide
　Your runkly measled shins, Callum ;
Lyart pow, as white's the tow,
　And beard as rough's the whins, Callum.

Wily woman aft deceives,
　Sae ye'll think, I ween, Callum ;
Trees may keep their withered leaves,
　Till ance they get green, Callum.
Blythe young Donald's won my heart
　Has my willing vow, Callum ;
Now, for a' your couthy art,
　I winna marry you, Callum.

Anacreontic.

FILL the merry bowl,
　Drown corrosive care and sorrow,
Why, why clog the soul,
　By caring for to-morrow ?
Fill your glasses, toast your lasses,
　Blythe Anacreon bids you live ;
Love with friendship far surpasses
　All the pleasure life can give.

Ring, ring the enlivening bell,
   The merry dirge of care and sorrow,
Why leave them life to tell
   Their heavy tales to-morrow ?

Come, join the social glee,
   Give the reins to festive pleasure ;
While fancy, light and free,
   Dances to the measure.
Love and wit, with all the graces,
   Revel round in fairy ring,
Smiling joy adorns our faces,
   While with jocund hearts we sing.

   Now, since our cares are drowned,
     Spite of what the sages tell us,
   Hoary time, in all his round,
     Ne'er saw such happy fellows.

Companion of my youthful sports.

Air—" Gilderoy."

COMPANION of my youthful sports,
   From love and friendship torn,
A victim to the pride of courts,
   Thy early death I mourn.
Unshrouded on a foreign shore,
   Thou'rt mouldering in the clay,
While here thy weeping friends deplore
   Corunna's fatal day.

How glows the youthful warrior's mind
   With thoughts of laurels won,
But ruthless ruin lurks behind,
   " And marks him for her own."
How soon the meteor ray is shed,
   " That lures him to his doom,"
And dark oblivion veils his head,
   In everlasting gloom !

The Soldier's Widow.

THE cold wind blows o'er the drifted snows,
  Loud howls the rain-washed naked wood,
Weary I stray on my lonesome way,
  And my heart is faint with want of food.
    Pity a wretch left all forlorn,
    On life's wide wintry waste to mourn ;
    The gloom of night fast veils the sky,
    And pleads for your humanity.

On valour's bed my Henry died,
  In the cheerless desert is his tomb :
Now lost to joy, with my little boy,
  In woe and want I wander home.
    Oh, never, never will you miss
    The boon bestowed on deep distress,
    For dear to Heaven is the glistening eye,
    That beams benign humanity.

———

One Night in my youth.

Air—"The lass that wears green."

ONE night in my youth as I roved with my merry pipe,
  Listening the echoes that rang to the tune,
I met Kitty More with her two lips so cherry ripe,
  Phelim, says she, give us Ellen Aroon !
Dear Kitty, says I, thou'rt so charmingly free !
  Now if thou wilt deign thy sweet voice to the measure
'Twill make all the echoes run giddy with pleasure,
  For none in fair Erin can sing it like thee.

My chanter I plied with my heart beating gaily,
  I piped up the strain, while so sweetly she sung ;
The soft melting melody filled all the valley,
  The green woods around us in harmony rung.
Methought that she verily charmed up the moon !
  Now, still, as I wander in village or city,
  When good people call for some favourite ditty,
    give them sweet Kitty, and Ellen Aroon.

Coggie, thou heals me.

DOROTHY sits i' the cauld ingle nook,
  Her red rosy neb's like a labster tae,
Wi' girnin' her mou's like the gab o' the fluke,
  Wi' smoking, her teeth's like the jet o' the slae.
And aye she sings weels me, aye she sings weels me,
Coggie, thou heals me ! coggie thou heals me !
Aye my best friend when there's onything ails me,
Ne'er shall we part till the day that I die.

Dorothy ance was a weel tochered lass,
  Had charms like her neighbours, and lovers enew,
But she spited them sae, wi' her pride and her sauce,
  They left her for thirty lang simmers to rue.
Then aye she sang waes me, aye she sang waes me,
Oh, I'll turn crazy, oh, I'll turn crazy,
Naething in a' the wide world can ease me,
De'il tak' the wooers, oh, what shall I do ?

Dorothy, dozen'd wi' living her lane,
  Pu'd at her rock, wi' the tear in her e'e ;
She thought on the braw merry days that were gane,
  And coft a wee coggie for company.
Now aye she sings weels me, aye she sings weels me,
Coggie, thou heals me ! coggie, thou heals me !
Aye my best friend when there's onything ails me,
Ne'er shall we part till the day that I die.

Ellen More.

THE sun had kissed green Erin's waves,
  The dark blue mountains towered between,
Mild evening's dews refreshed the leaves,
  The moon unclouded rose serene,
When Ellen wandered forth unseen,
  All lone her sorrows to deplore ;
False was her lover, false her friend,
  And false was hope to Ellen More.

Young Henry was fair Ellen's love,
  Young Emma to her heart was dear ;

Nor weal nor woe did Ellen prove,
　　But Emma ever seemed to share :
Yet envious still, she spread the wile,
　　That sullied Ellen's virtues o'er ;
Her faithless Henry spurned the while,
　　His fair, his faithful Ellen More.

She wandered down Loch-Mary side,
　　Where oft at evening hour she stole,
To meet her love with secret pride ;
　　Now deepest anguish wrung her soul.
O'ercome with grief, she sought the steep
　　Where Yarrow falls with sullen roar ;
Oh, pity ! veil thy eyes and weep,
　　A bleeding corpse lies Ellen More.

The sun may shine on Yarrow braes,
　　And woo the mountain flowers to bloom,
But never can his golden rays
　　Awake the flower in yonder tomb :
There oft young Henry strays forlorn,
　　When moonlight gilds the abbey tower ;
There oft from eve till breezy morn,
　　He weeps his faithful Ellen More.

Green Inismore.

Air—"The Leitrim County."

How light is my heart as we journey along,
　　Now my perilous service is o'er,
I think on sweet home, and I carol a song,
　　In remembrance of her I adore ;
How sad was the hour when I bid her adieu !
Her tears spoke her grief, though her words were but few ;
She hung on my bosom, and sighed, Oh, be true,
　　When you're far from the green Inismore !

Ah, Eveleen, my love, hadst thou seen this fond breast,
　　How, at parting, it bled to its core,
Thou hadst there seen thine image so deeply impressed,
　　That thou ne'er couldst have doubted me more.

For my king and my country undaunted I fought,
And braved all the hardships of war as I ought,
But the day never rose saw thee strange to my thought
  Since I left thee in green Inismore.

Ye dear native mountains that tower in my view,
  What joys to my mind ye restore ;
The past happy scenes to my life ye renew,
  And ye ne'er seemed so charming before.
In the rapture of fancy already I spy
My kindred and friends crowding round me with joy,
But my Eveleen, sweet girl, there's a far dearer tie,
  Binds this heart to the green Inismore.

The Midges Dance Aboon the Burn.

THE midges dance aboon the burn,
  The dews begin to fa',
The paitricks down the rushy holm
  Set up their evening ca'.
Now loud and clear the blackbird's sang
  Rings through the briery shaw,
While flitting gay, the swallows play
  Around the castle wa'.

Beneath the golden gloaming sky,
  The mavis mends her lay,
The redbreast pours his sweetest strains,
  To charm the lingering day :
While weary yeldrins seem to wail
  Their little nestlings torn,
The merry wren, frae den to den,
  Gaes jinking through the thorn.

The roses fauld their silken leaves,
  The foxglove shuts its bell,
The honeysuckle and the birk
  Spread fragrance through the dell.
Let others crowd the giddy court
  Of mirth and revelry,
The simple joys that nature yields
  Are dearer far to me.

Gloomy Winter's now awa'.

Air—"Lord Balgounie's Favourite."

Gloom - y Win - ter's now a - wa', Saft the west - lin' breez - es blaw;

'Mang the birks o' Stan - ley shaw The ma - vis sings fu' cheer-ie, O.

Sweet the craw-flower's ear - ly bell, Decks Glen - if - fer's dew - y dell,

Bloom-ing like thy bon - nie sel', My young, my art - less dear - ie, O.

Come, my las - sie, let us stray, O'er Glen - kil-loch's sun - ny brae,

Blyth - ly spend the gow - den day, 'Mid'st joys that nev - er wear - ry, O.

Tow'ring o'er the Newton woods,
Lav'rocks fan the snaw-white clouds,
Siller saughs, wi' downy buds,
   Adorn the bank, sae briery, O.
Round the sylvan fairy nooks,
Feath'ry breckans fringe the rocks,
'Neath the brae the burnie jouks,
   And ilka thing is cheerie, O.
Trees may bud, and birds may sing,
Flowers may bloom, and verdure spring,
Joy to me they canna bring,
    Unless with thee, my dearie, O.

D

The Wandering Bard.

CHILL the wintry winds were blowing,
Foul the murky night was snowing,
Through the storm, the minstrel, bowing,
   Sought the inn on yonder moor:
All within was warm and cheerie,
All without was cold and dreary,
There the wanderer, old and weary,
   Thought to pass the night secure.

Softly rose his mournful ditty,
Suiting to his tale of pity;
But the master, scoffing witty,
   Checked his strain with scornful jeer:
" Hoary vagrant, frequent comer,
Canst thou guide thy gains of summer?
No, thou old intruding thrummer,
   Thou canst have no lodging here."

Slow the bard departed, sighing;
Wounded worth forbade replying;
One last feeble effort trying,
   Faint he sunk, no more to rise;
Through his harp, the breeze sharp ringing,
Wild his dying dirge was singing,
While his soul, from insult springing,
   Sought its mansion in the skies.

Now, though wintry winds be blowing,
Night be foul, with raining, snowing,
Still the traveller, that way going,
   Shuns the inn upon the moor.
Though within 'tis warm and cheerie,
Though without 'tis cold and dreary,
Still he minds the minstrel weary,
   Spurned from that unfriendly door,

Winter wi' his Cloudy Brow.

Air—"Forneth house."

Now winter wi' his cloudy brow,
  Is far ayont yon mountains,
And spring beholds her azure sky
  Reflected in the fountains.
Now on the budding slacthorn bank,
  She spreads her early blossom,
And woos the mirly-breasted birds
  To nestle in her bosom.
But lately a' was clad wi' snaw,
  Sae darksome, dull, and dreary,
Now laverocks sing to hail the spring,
  And nature a' is cheerie.

Then let us leave the town, my love,
  And seek our country dwelling,
Where waving woods and spreading flowers,
  On every side are smiling.
We'll tread again the daisied green,
  Where first your beauty moved me;
We'll trace again the woodland scene,
  Where first ye owned ye loved me:
We soon will view the roses blaw
  In a' the charms of fancy;
For doubly dear these pleasures a',
  When shared with thee, my Nancy.

Fragment of a Scottish Ballad.

Air—"Fingal's lamentation."

WILD drives the bitter northern blast,
  Fierce whirling wide the crispy snaw,
Young lassie, turn your wandering steps,
  For evening's gloom begins to fa'.
I'll tak' you to my father's ha',
  And shield you from the wintry air;
For wandering through the drifting snaw,
  I fear you'll sink to rise nae mair.

Ah! gentle lady, airt my way
  Across this langsome lonely moor,

For he wha's dearest to my heart,
  Now waits me on the western shore.
With morn he spreads his outward sail,
  This night I vowed to meet him there,
To take ae secret fond fareweel ;
  We maybe part to meet nae mair.

Dear lassie, turn ! 'twill be your dead ?
  The dreary waste lies far and wide ;
Abide till morn, and then ye'll ha'e
  My father's herdboy for your guide.
No, lady, no ! I maunna turn,
  Impatient love now chides my stay ;
Yon rising moon, with kindly beam,
  Will light me on my weary way.

  *   *   *   *   *

Ah ! Donald, wherefore bounds thy heart ?
  Why beams with joy thy wishful e'e ?
Yon's but thy true love's fleeting form,
  Thy true love mair thou'lt never see.
Deep in the hollow glen she lies,
  Amang the snaw, beneath the tree ;
She soundly sleeps in death's cauld arms,
  A victim to her love for thee.

Ah! Sheelah, thou'rt my Darling.

Air—" Nancy Verny."

Ah ! Sheelah, thou'rt my darling,
  The golden image of my heart,
How cheerless seems this morning,
  It brings the hour when we must part :
Though doomed to cross the ocean,
  And face the proud insulting foe,
Thou hast my soul's devotion,
  My heart is thine where'er I go !
Ah, Sheelah, thou'rt my darling,
  My heart is thine where'er I go !
When tossed upon the billow,
  And angry tempests round me blow,

Let not the gloomy willow
　　O'ershade thy lovely lily brow ;
But mind the seaman's story,
　　Sweet William and his charming Sue ;
I'll soon return with glory,
　　And, like sweet William, wed thee too.
Ah, Sheelah, thou'rt my darling,
　　My heart is thine where'er I go !

Think on our days of pleasure,
　　While wandering by the Shannon side,
When summer days gave leisure
　　To stray amidst their flowery pride ;
And while thy faithful lover
　　Is far upon the stormy main,
Think, when the wars are over,
　　These golden days shall come again !
Ah, Sheelah, thou'rt my darling,
　　These golden days shall come again !

Farewell, ye lofty mountains,
　　Your flowery wilds we wont to rove ;
Ye woody glens and fountains,
　　The dear retreats of mutual love.
Alas, we now must sever ;
　　Oh, Sheelah, to thy vows be true,
My heart is thine for ever ;
　　One fond embrace, and then adieu !
Ah, Sheelah, thou'rt my darling,
　　One fond embrace, and then adieu !

Molly, my dear.

THE harvest is o'er, and the lads are so funny,
Their hearts lined with love, and their pockets with money,
From morning till night 'tis " My jewel, my honey,
　　Och, go to the north with me, Molly, my dear."
Young Dermot holds on with his sweet botheration,
And swears there is only one flower in the nation ;
" Thou rose of the Shannon, thou pink of creation,
　　Och, go to the north with me, Molly, my dear."

"The sun courts thy smiles as he sinks in the ocean,
The moon to thy charms veils her face in devotion,
And I my poor self, och, so rich is my notion,
  Would pay down the world for sweet Molly, my dear."

Though Thady can match all the lads with his blarney,
And sings me love-songs of the lakes of Killarney,
In worth from my Dermot he's twenty miles' journey,
  My heart bids me tell him I'll ne'er be his dear.

Peggy O'Rafferty.

Air—"Paddy O'Rafferty."

On, could I fly like the green-coated fairy,
I'd skip o'er the ocean to dear Tipperary,
Where all the young fellows are blythesome and merry,
  While here I lament my sweet Peggy O'Rafferty.
How could I bear in my bosom to leave her,
In absence I think her more lovely than ever ;
With thoughts of her beauty I'm all in a fever,
  Since others may woo my sweet Peggy O'Rafferty.

Scotland, thy lasses are modest and bonnie,
But here every Jennie has got her own Johnnie,
And though I might call them my jewel and honey,
  My heart is at home with sweet Peggy O'Rafferty :
Wistful I think on my dear native mountains,
Their green shady glens and their crystalline fountains,
And ceaseless I heave the deep sigh of repentance,
  That ever I left my sweet Peggy O'Rafferty.

Fortune, 'twas thine all the light foolish notion,
That led me to rove o'er the wide rolling ocean,
But what now to me all the hopes of promotion,
  Since I am so far from sweet Peggy O'Rafferty.
Grant me as many thirteens as will carry
Me down through the country and over the ferry,
I'll hie me straight home into dear Tipperary,
  And never more leave my sweet Peggy O'Rafferty.

Ye Friendly Stars.

Air—"Gamby Ora."

YE friendly stars that rule the night,
  And hail my glad returning,
Ye never shone so sweetly bright,
  Since gay St. Patrick's morning.
My life hung heavy on my mind,
  Despair sat brooding o'er me;
Now all my cares are full behind,
  And joy is full before me.
      Gamby ora, gamby ora,
        How my heart approves me;
      Gamby ora, gamby ora,
        Kathleen owns she loves me.

Were all the flowery pastures mine,
  That deck fair Limerick county,
That wealth, dear Kathleen, should be thine,
  And all should share our bounty:
But fortune's gifts I value not,
  Nor grandeur's highest station;
I would not change my happy lot
  For all the Irish nation.
      Gamby ora, gamby ora, &c.

The Defeat.

FROM hill to hill the bugles sound
  The soul-arousing strain,
The war-bred coursers paw the ground,
  And foaming, champ the rein.
Their steel-clad riders bound on high,
  A bold defensive host;
With valour fired, away they fly,
  Like lightning, to the coast.

And now they view the wide-spread lines
  Of the invading foe;
Now skill with British bravery joins,
  To strike one final blow.

Now on they rush with giant stroke ;
   Ten thousand victims bleed ;
They trample on the iron yoke
   Which France for us decreed.

Now view the trembling vanquished crew
   Kneel o'er their prostrate arms,
Implore respite of vengeance due
   For all these dire alarms.
Now, while humanity's warm glow,
   Half weeps the guilty slain,
Let conquest gladden every brow,
   And godlike mercy reign.

Thus fancy paints that awful day :
   Yes, dreadful, should it come ;
But Britain's sons, in stern array,
   Shall brave its darkest gloom.
Who fights, his native rights to save,
   His worth shall have its claim ;
The bard will consecrate his grave,
   And give his name to fame.

Adieu, ye cheerful native plains.

Air—" The green woods of Treugh."

ADIEU, ye cheerful native plains,
   Dungeon glooms receive me,
Nought, alas, for me remains,
   Of all the joys ye gave me.
      All are flown !
Banished from thy shores, sweet Erin,
I through life must toil despairing,
      Lost and unknown.

Howl, ye winds ! around my cell,
   Nothing now can wound me ;
Mingling with your dreary swell,
   Prison groans surround me :
      Bodings wild !
Treachery, thy ruthless doing,
Long I'll mourn in hopeless ruin,
      Lost and exiled !

The Dirge of Carolan.

[Carolan is the most celebrated of all the modern Irish bards. He was born in the village of Nobber, County of Westmeath, 1670, and died in 1739. He never regretted the loss of his sight, but used gaily to say, "My eyes are only transported into my ears." It has been said of his music, by O'Connor, the celebrated historian, who knew him intimately, that so happy, so elevated was he in some of his compositions, he attained the approbation of that great master, Geminina, who never saw him. His execution, too, on the harp, was rapid and impressive, far beyond that of all the professional competitors of the age in which he lived. The charms of woman, the pleasures of conviviality, and the power of poetry and music, were at once his theme and inspiration; and his life was an illustration of his theory; for until his last ardour was chilled by death, he loved, drank, and sung. While in the fervour of composition, he was constantly heard to pass sentence on his own effusions, as they rose on his harp, or breathed from his lips: blaming and praising, with equal vehemence, the unsuccessful effort and felicitous attempt. He was the welcome guest of every house, from the peasant to the prince, but in the true wandering spirit of his profession, he never stayed to exhaust that welcome. He lived and died poor.—LADY MORGAN.]

Air—"Ballymoney."

YE maids of green Erin, why sigh ye so sad?
The summer is smiling, all nature is glad.
The summer may smile, and the shamrock may bloom,
But the pride of green Erin lies cold in the tomb;
And his merits demand all the tears that we shed,
Though they ne'er can awaken the slumbering dead;
Yet still they shall flow—for dear Carolan we mourn,
For the soul of sweet music now sleeps in his urn.

Ye bards of our isle, join our grief with your songs,
For the deepest regret to his memory belongs;
In our cabins and fields, on our mountains and plains,
How oft have we sung to his sweet melting strains.
Ah! these strains shall survive, long as time they shall last,
Yet they now but remind us of joys that are past;
And our days, crowned with pleasure, can never return,
For the soul of sweet music now sleeps in his urn.

Yes, thou pride of green Erin! thy honours thoul't have,
Seven days, seven nights, we shall weep round thy grave;
And thy harp that so oft to our ditties has rung,
To the lorn-sighing breeze o'er thy grave shall be hung;
And the song shall ascend thy bright worth to proclaim,
That thy shade may rejoice in the voice of thy fame;
But our days, crowned with pleasure, can never return,
For the soul of sweet music now sleeps in thine urn.

My Mary.

Air—" Invercauld's reel."

My Mary is a bonnie lassie,
  Sweet as dewy morn,
When fancy tunes her rural reed
  Beside the upland thorn.
She lives ahint yon sunny knowe,
Where flowers in wild profusion grow,
Where spreading birks and hazels throw
  Their shadows owre the burn.

'Tis no the streamlet-skirted wood,
  Wi' a' its leafy bowers,
That gars me wait in solitude
  Among the wild spring flowers ;
But aft I cast a langing e'e,
Down frae the bank, out owre the lea,
There, haply, I my lass may see,
  As through the broom she scours.

Yestreen I met my bonnie lassie
  Comin frae the town,
We raptured sunk in ither's arms,
  And pressed the breckans down :
The paitrick sung his e'ening note,
  The rye craik risped his clamorous throat,
While there the heavenly vow I got,
  That earled her my own.

————

Oh, Row thee in my Highland Plaid.

Lowland lassie wilt thou go
Where the hills are clad with snow ;
Where, beneath the icy steep,
The hardy shepherd tends his sheep ?
Ill nor wae shall thee betide,
When rowed within my Highland plaid.

Soon the voice of cheerie spring
Will gar a' our plantin's ring ;
Soon our bonnie heather braes,
Will put on their simmer claes :

On the mountain's sunny side,
We'll lean us on my Highland plaid.

When the simmer spreads the flowers,
Busks the glen in leafy bowers,
Then we'll seek the caller shade,
Lean us on the primrose bed;
While the burning hours preside,
I'll screen thee wi' my Highland plaid.

Then we'll leave the sheep and goat,
I will launch the bonnie boat,
Skim the loch in canty glee,
Rest the oars to pleasure thee.
When chilly breezes sweep the tide,
I'll hap thee wi' my Highland plaid.

Lowland lads may dress mair fine,
Woo in words mair saft than mine;
Lowland lads ha'e mair of art,
A' my boast's an honest heart,
Whilk shall ever be my pride:
Oh, row thee in my Highland plaid!

Bonnie lad, ye've been sae leal,
My heart would break at our fareweel,
Lang your love has made me fain:
Tak' me, tak' me for your ain!
'Cross the frith away they glide,
Young Donald and his Lowland bride.

Responsive, ye Woods.
Air—" My time, O ye muses."

RESPONSIVE, ye woods, wing your echoes along,
Till nature, all sad, weeping, listen my song,
Till flocks cease their bleating, and herds cease to low,
And the clear winding rivulet scarce seems to flow.
For fair was the flower that once gladdened our plains,
Sweet rosebud of virtue, adored by our swains;
But fate, like a blast, from the chill wintry wave,
Has laid my sweet flower in yon cold silent grave.

Her warm feeling breast did with sympathy glow,
In innocence pure as the new mountain snow;

Her face was more fair than the mild apple bloom,
Her voice sweet as hope, whispering pleasures to come.
Oh, Mary, my love, wilt thou never return?
'Tis thy William who calls! burst the bands of thy urn!
Together we'll wander—poor wretch, how I rave!
My Mary lies low in the lone silent grave.

Yon tall leafy planes throw a deep solemn shade
O'er the dear holy spot where my Mary is laid,
Lest the light wanton sunbeams obtrude on the gloom,
That lorn love and friendship have wove round her tomb.
Still there let the mild tears of nature remain,
Till calm dewy evening weep o'er her again;
There oft I will wander—no boon now I crave,
But to weep life away o'er the dark silent grave.

Ye dear romantic Shades.

Air—"Mrs. Hamilton of Wishaw's strathspey."

Far from the giddy court of mirth,
    Where sickening follies reign,
By Levern banks I wander forth
    To hail each sylvan scene.
All hail, ye dear romantic shades!
Ye banks, ye woods, and sunny glades!
Here oft the musing poet treads
    In Nature's riches great:
Contrast the country with the town,
Makes Nature's beauties all his own;
And, borne on fancy's wings, looks down
    On empty pride and state.

By dewy dawn, or sultry noon,
    Or sober evening gray,
I'll often quit the dinsome town,
    By Levern banks to stray:
Or from the uplands mossy brow
Enjoy the fancy-pleasing view
Of streamlets, woods, and fields below,
    A sweetly varied scene.
Give riches to the miser's care,
Let folly shine in fashion's glare,
Give me the wealth of peace and health,
    With all their happy train.

Though humble my lot.

Air—"Her sheep had in clusters."

WHERE primroses spring on the green-tufted brae,
  And the rivulet runs murmuring below,
Oh, fortune! at morning, or noon, let me stray,
  And thy wealth on thy votaries bestow:
For, oh! how enraptured my bosom does glow
  As calmly I wander alone,
Where wild woods, and bushes, and primroses grow,
  And a streamlet enlivens the scene.

Though humble my lot, not ignoble's my state,
  Let me still be contented though poor;
What destiny brings, be resigned to my fate,
  Though misfortune should knock at my door.
I care not for honour, preferment, nor wealth,
  For the title that affluence yields,
While blythely I roam in the heyday of health,
  'Midst the charms of my dear native fields.

Bonnie winsome Mary.

Gaelic Air.

FORTUNE, frowning most severe,
Forced me from my native dwelling,
Parting with my friends so dear,
Cost me many a bitter tear:
But, like the clouds of early day,
Soon my sorrows fled away,
When, blooming sweet and smiling,
I met my winsome Mary.

Wha can sit with gloomy brow,
Blessed with sic a charming lassie?
Native scenes, I think on you,
Yet the change I canna rue;
Wandering many a weary mile,
Now fortune seemed to lower the while,
But she's gi'en me, for the toil,
My bonnie winsome Mary.

Though our riches are but few,
Faithful love is aye a treasure ;
Ever cheerie, kind, and true,
Nane but her I e'er can lo'e.
Hear me, a' ye powers above,
Powers of sacred truth and love!
While I live I'll constant prove
To my dear winsome Mary.

The Maniac's Song.

HARK ! 'tis the poor maniac's song ;
    She sits on yon wild craggy steep,
And while the winds mournfully whistle along,
    She wistfully looks o'er the deep :
And aye she sings, " Lullaby, lullaby, lullaby !"
    To hush the rude billows asleep.

She looks to yon rock far at sea,
    And thinks it her lover's white sail ;
The warm tear of joy glads her wild glistening e'e,
    As she reckons his vessel to hail ;
And aye she sings " Lullaby, lullaby, lullaby !"
    And frets at the boisterous gale.

Poor Susan was gentle and fair,
    'Till the seas robbed her heart of its joy ;
Then her reason was lost in the gloom of despair,
    And her charms then did wither and die :
And now her sad "lullaby, lullaby, lullaby !"
    Oft wakes the lone passenger's sigh.

Ye Echoes that Ring.

YE echoes that ring round the woods of Bowgreen,
    Say, did ye e'er listen sae melting a strain,
When lovely young Jessie gaed wandering unseen,
    And sung of her laddie, the pride of the plain.
Aye she sung, Willie, my bonnie young Willie !
There's no a sweet flower on the mountain or valley,
Mild blue spritled crowflower, or wild woodland lily,
    But tines a' its sweets in my bonny young swain.

Thou goddess of love, keep him constant to me.
Else, withering in sorrow, poor Jessie shall die !

Her laddie had strayed through the dark leafy wood,
 His thoughts were a' fixed on his dear lassie's charms,
He heard her sweet voice, all transported he stood,
 'Twas the soul of his wishes—he flew to her arms,
No, my dear Jessie ! my lovely young Jessie !
Through summer, through winter, I'll doat and caress thee,
Thou'rt dearer than life ! thou'rt my ae only lassie !
 Then, banish thy bosom these needless alarms,
Yon red setting sun sooner changeful shall be,
Ere wavering in falsehood I wander frae thee.

The Negro Girl.

Yon poor negro girl, an exotic plant,
 Was torn from her dear native soil ;
Reluctantly borne o'er the raging Atlant,
 Then brought to Britannia's isle.
Though Fatima's mistress be loving and kind,
 Poor Fatima still must deplore ;
She thinks on her parents, left weeping behind,
 And sighs for her dear native shore.

She thinks on her Zadi, the youth of her heart,
 Who from childhood was loving and true ;
How he cried on the beach when the ship did depart ?
 'Twas a sad everlasting adieu.
The shell-woven gift which he bound round her arm,
 The rude seaman unfeelingly tore,
Nor left one sad relic her sorrows to charm,
 When far from her dear native shore.

And now, all dejected, she wanders apart,
 No friend save retirement she seeks ;
The sigh of despondency bursts from her heart,
 And tears dew her thin sable cheeks.
Poor hard-fated girl, long, long she may mourn !
 Life's pleasure's to her all are o'er ;
Far fled every hope that she e'er should return
 To revisit her dear native shore.

My heart is sair wi' heavy care.

Air—"The rosy brier."

My heart is sair wi' heavy care,
  To think on friendship's fickle smile ;
It blinks a wee wi' kindly e'e,
  When world's thrift runs weel the while.
But let misfortune's tempests lower,
It soon turns cold, it soon turns sour ;
  It looks sae high and scornfully,
It winna ken a poor man's door.

I ance had siller in my purse,
  I dealt it out right frank and free,
And hoped, should fortune change her course,
  That they would do the same for me :
But, weak in wit, I little thought
That friendship's smiles were sold and bought,
  Till ance I saw, like April suaw,
They waned awa' when I had nought.

It's no to see my threadbare coat,
  It's no to see my coggie toom,
It's no to wair my hindmost groat,
  That gars me fret and gars me gloom :
But 'tis to see the scornful pride
That honest poortith aft maun bide
    Frae selfish slaves, and sordid knaves,
  What strut with fortune on their side.

But let it gang, what de'il care I !
  Wi' cydent thrift I'll toil for mair ;
I'll half my mite with misery,
  But fient a ane o' them shall share.
With soul unbent I'll stand the stour,
And while they're fluttering past my door,
  I'll sing with glee and let them see
An honest heart can ne'er be poor.

Bonnie Wood of Craigielee.

The broom, the brier, the bir-ken bush, Bloom bon-nie o'er thy flow'ry lea; And

a' the sweets that ane can wish, Frae na-ture's hand are strewed on thee.

Thou bon-nie wood of Craig-ie-l e, Thou bon-nie wood of Craig-ie-lee, Near

thee I've spent life's ear-ly day, And won my Ma-ry's heart in thee.

Far ben thy dark green plantin's shade,
The cushat croodles am'rously,
The mavis down thy bughted glade,
Gars echo ring frae ev'ry tree.
Thou bonnie wood, &c.

Awa', ye thoughtless murd'ring gang,
Wha tear the nestlings ere they flee!
They'll sing you yet a canty sang,
Then, oh! in pity let them be!
Thou bonnie wood, &c.

When winter blaws in sleety showers,
Frae aff the norlan' hills sae hie,
He lightly skiffs thy bonnie bow'rs,
As laith to harm a flow'r in thee.
Thou bonnie wood, &c.

Though fate should drive me south the line,
Or o'er the wide Atlantic sea,
The happy hours I'll ever min',
That I in youth ha'e spent in thee.
Thou bonnie wood, &c.

E

I marked a Gem of Pearly Dew.

I MARKED a gem of pearly dew,
　　While wandering near yon misty mountain,
Which bore the tender flower so low,
　　It dropped off into the fountain.
So thou hast wrung this gentle heart,
　　Which in its core was proud to wear thee,
Till, drooping sick beneath thy art,
　　It sighing found it could not bear thee !

Adieu, thou faithless fair ! unkind !
　　Thy falsehood dooms that we must sever ;
Thy vows were as the passing wind,
　　That fans the flower, then dies for ever.
And think not that this gentle heart,
　　Though in its core 'twas proud to wear thee,
Shall longer droop beneath thy art ;
　　No, cruel fair ! it cannot bear thee !

The Bard of Glenullin.

THOUGH my eyes are grown dim, and my locks are turned
　　　　grey,
I feel not the storms of life's bleak wintry day,
For my cot is well thatched, and my barns are full stored,
And cheerful content still presides at my board :
Warm-hearted benevolence stands at my door,
Dispensing her gifts to the wandering poor ;
The glow of the heart does my bounty repay,
And lightens the heart of life's bleak wintry day.

From the summit of years I look down on the vale,
Where age pines in sorrow, neglected and pale :
Where the sunshine of fortune scarce deigns to bestow
One heart-cheering smile to the wand'rers below.
From the sad dreary prospect this lesson I drew,
That those who are helpless are friended by few,
So with vigorous industry I smoothed the rough way
That leads through the vale of life's bleak wintry day.

Then, my son, let the bard of Glenullin advise,
For years can give counsel, experience makes wise ;
'Midst thy wanderings let honour for aye be thy guide.
O'er thy actions let honesty ever preside.
Then, though hardships assail thee, in virtue thoul't smile,
For light is the heart that's untainted with guile;
But, if fortune attend thee, my counsels obey,
Prepare for the storms of life's bleak wintry day,

The Coggie.

Air—" Cauld kail in Aberdeen."

WHEN poortith cauld, and sour disdain,
   Hang owre life's vale sae foggie,
The sun that brightens up the scene,
   Is friendship's kindly coggie.
      Then, oh revere the coggie, sirs !
      The friendly social coggie !
      It gars the wheels of life run light,
      Though e'er so doilt and cloggie.

Let pride in fortune's chariots fly,
   Sae empty, vain, and voggie ;
The source of wit, the spring of joy,
   Lies in the social coggie.
      Then, oh ! revere the coggie, sirs !
      The independent coggie !
      And never smool beneath the frown
      Of ony selfish roggie.

Poor modest worth, wi' cheerless e'e,
   Sits hurkling in the boggie,
Till she asserts her dignity,
   By virtue of the coggie.
      Then, oh ! revere the coggie, sirs !
      The poor man's patron coggie,
      It warsels care, it fights life's faughts,
      And lifts him frae the boggie.

Gi'e feckless Spain her weak snail broo,
　　Gi'e France her weel-spiced froggie,
Gi'e brother John his luncheon too,
　　But gi'e to us our coggie.
　　　　Then, oh! revere the coggie, sirs,
　　　　Our soul-warm kindred coggie;
　　　　Hearts doubly knit in social tie,
　　　　When just a wee thought groggie.

In days of yore our sturdy sires,
　　Upon their hills sae scroggie,
Glowed with true freedom's warmest fires,
　　And fought to save their coggie.
　　　　Then, oh! revere the coggie, sirs,
　　　　Our brave forefathers' coggie;
　　　　It roused them up to doughty deeds,
　　　　O'er which we'll lang be vogie.

Then here's may Scotland ne'er fa' down,
　　A cringing, coward doggie,
But bauldly stand and bang the loon,
　　Wha'd reave her of her coggie!
　　　　Then, oh! protect the coggie, sirs, ·
　　　　Our good auld mother's coggie!
　　　　Nor let her luggie e'er be drained
　　　　By any foreign roggie.

———

Davie Tulloch's Bonnie Katy.

DAVIE TULLOCH's bonnie Katy,
　　Davie's bonnie, blythesome Katy,
Tam the laird cam' down yestreen,
　　He sought her love, but gat her pity.
Wi' trembling grip he squeezed her hand,
　　While his auld heart gaed pitty-patty;
Aye he thought his gear and land
　　Wad win the love o' bonnie Katy.

Davie Tulloch's bonnie Katy,
　　Davie's bonnie, blythesome Katy;
Aye she smiled as Davie wiled:
　　Her smile was scorn, yet mixed wi' pity.

Oh, laddie, can you leave me?

OH, laddie, can you leave me?
    Alas, 'twill break this constant heart;
There's nought on earth can grieve me
    Like this, that we must part:
Think on the tender vow you made
    Beneath the secret birken shade;
And can you now deceive me!
    Is a' your love but art?

I'll lay me on the wintry lea.

I'LL lay me on the wintry lea,
    And sleep amidst the wind and weet;
And ere another's bride I be,
    Oh, bring me to my winding sheet?
What can a helpless lassie do,
    When ilka friend wad prove a foe:
Wad gar her break her dearest vow,
    To wed wi' ane she canna lo'e?

Fair-haired Nanny.

FULL eighteen summers up life's brae,
    I speeded on fu' canny, O,
Till sleeky love threw in my way
    Young bonnie fair-haired Nanny, O.
I wooed her soon, I won her syne,
    Our vows o' love were many, O;
And, oh! what happy days were mine,
    Wi' bonnie fair-haired Nannie, O.

Were ye at Duntocher Burn.

AND were ye at Duntocher burn?
    And did ye see them a', man?
And how's my wifie and the bairns?
    I ha'e been lang awa', man.

This hedger wark's a weary trade,
　　It doesna suit ava', man ;
Wi' lanely house and lanely bed
　　My comforts are but sma', man.

Cauld gloomy Feberwar.

Thou cauld gloomy Feberwar,
　　Oh, gin thou wert awa';
I'm wae to hear thy soughing winds,
　　I'm wae to see thy snaw :
For my bonnie brave young Highlander,
　　The lad I lo'e so dear,
Has vowed to come and see me,
　　In the spring o' the year.

Marion, dry your tearfu' e'e.

Now Marion, dry your tearfu' e'e,
　　Gae break your rock in twa,
For soon your gallant sons ye'll see,
　　Returned in safety a'.
Oh, vow, guidman, my heart is fain !
And shall I see my bairns again ?
A' seated round our ain hearthstane,
　　Nae mair to gang awa' ?

Come hame to your lingels.

Air—" Whistle and I'll come to you, my lad."

Come hame to your lingels, ye ne'er-do-weel loon,
You're the king of the dyvours, the talk o' the town ;
Sae soon as the Munonday morning comes in,
Your wearifu' daidling again maun begin !
Guidwife, ye're a skillet, your tongue's just a bell,
To the peace o' guid fellows it brings the death-knell ;
But clack till ye deafen auld Barnaby's mill,
The souter shall aye ha'e his Munonday's yill.

Come hame to your lapstane, come hame to your last,
It's a bonnie affair that your family maun fast,
While you and your crew here a guzzling maun sit,
Ye dazed, drunken, guid-for-nocht heir o' the pit :
Just look, how I'm gaun without stocking or shoe,
Your bairns a' in tatters, and fatherless too,
And yet, quite content, like a sot, ye'll sit still,
Till your kyte's like to crack, wi' your Mononday's yill.

I'll tell you, guidwife, gin ye haudna your clack,
I'll lend you a reestle wi' this, owre your back ;
Maun we be abused and affronted by you,
Wi' sican foul names as loon, dyvour, and crew ?
Come hame to your lingels, this instant come hame,
Or I'll redden your face, gin ye've yet ony shame,
For I'll bring a' the bairns, and we'll just ha'e our fill,
As weel as yoursel', o' your Mononday's yill.

Gin that be the gate o't, sirs, come let us stir,
What need we sit here to be pestered by her ?
For she'll plague and affront us as far as she can :
Did ever a woman sae bother a man ?
Frae yill-house to yill-house she'll after us rin,
And raise the whole town wi' her yelpin' an' din ;
Come ! ca' the guidwife, bid her bring in her bill :
I see I maun quat takin' Mononday's yill.

When Rosie was faithful.

Written on reading " The Harper of Mull," a Highland story.

WHEN Rosie was faithful, how happy was I,
Still gladsome as summer the time glided by ;
I played my harp cheerie, while fondly I sang
Of the charms of my Rosie the winter nights lang.
But now I'm as waefu' as waefu' can be,
Come summer, come winter, 'tis a' ane to me :
For the dark gloom of falsehood sae clouds my sad soul,
That cheerless for aye is the harper of Mull.

I wander the glens and the wild woods alane,
In their deepest recesses I make my sad mane ;
My harp's mournful melody joins in the strain,
While sadly I sing of the days that are gane.

Though Rosie is faithless, she's no the less fair,
And the thought of her beauty but feeds my despair;
With painful remembrance my bosom is full,
And weary of life is the harper of Mull.

As slumbering I lay by the dark mountain stream,
My lovely young Rosie appeared in my dream:
I thought her still kind, and I ne'er was sae blessed,
As in fancy I clasped the dear nymph to my breast.
Thou false fleeting vision, too soon thou wert o'er,
Thou wak'dst me to tortures unequalled before;
But death's silent slumbers my griefs soon shall lull,
And the green grass wave over the harper of Mull.

Why Unite to Banish Care.

Why unite to banish care?
Let him come our joys to share;
Doubly blessed our cup shall flow,
When it soothes a brother's woe;
'Twas for this the powers divine
Crowned our board with generous wine.

Far be hence the sordid elf
Who'd claim enjoyment for himself;
Come, the hardy seaman, lame,
The gallant soldier robbed of fame,
Welcome all who bear the woes
Of various kind that merit knows.

" Patriot heroes, doomed to sigh
Idle 'neath corruption's eye;
Honest tradesmen, credit worn,
Pining under fortune's scorn,
Wanting wealth, or lacking fame,
Welcome all that worth can claim.

" Come, the hoary-headed sage,
Suffering more from want than age;
Come the proud, though needy bard,
Serving 'midst a world's regard:
Welcome, welcome, one and all
That feel on this unfeeling ball."

Brave Lewie Roy.

Gaelic air.

BRAVE Lewie Roy was the flower of our Highlandmen,
    Tall as the oak on the lofty Benvoirlich,
Fleet as the light-bounding tenants of Fillin glen,
    Dearer than life to his lovely *neen voiuch* *
Lone was his biding, the cave of his hiding,
    When forced to retire with our gallant Prince Charlie,
Though manly and fearless, his bold heart was cheerless,
    Away from the lady he aye loved so dearly.

" But woe on the bloodthirsty mandates of Cumberland,
    Woe on the bloodthirsty gang that fulfilled them ;
Poor Caledonia ! bleeding and plunder'd land,
    Where shall thy children now shelter and shield them ?
Keen prowl the cravens like merciless ravens,
    Their prey the devoted adherents of Charlie ;
Brave Lewie Roy is ta'en, cowardly hacked and slain,
    Ah ! his *neen voiuch* will mourn for him sairly."

My Dear Highland Laddie, O.

Air—" Morneen I gaberland."

BLYTHE was the time when he fee'd wi' my father, O.
Happy were the days when we herded thegither, O,
Sweet were the hours when he rowed me in his plaidie, O,
And vowed to be mine, my dear Highland laddie, O.

But ah ! waes me ! wi' their sodgering sae gaudy, O,
The laird's wysed awa' my braw Highland laddie, O,
Misty are the glens, and the dark hills sae cloudy, O,
That aye seemed sae blythe wi' my dear Highland laddie, O.

The blaeberry banks now are lonesome and dreary, O,
Muddy are the streams that gushed down sae clearly, O,
Silent are the rocks that echoed sae gladly, O,
The wild melting strains of my dear Highland laddie, O.

    * Beautiful maid.

Farewell my ewes ! and farewell my doggie, O,
Farewell ye knowes ! now sae cheerless and scroggie, O,
Farewell Glenfeoch ! my mammie and my daddie,, O
I will lea' you a' for my dear Highland laddie, O.

Lang Syne, beside the Woodland Burn.

LANG syne, beside the woodland burn,
  Amang the broom sae yellow,
I leaned me 'neath the milkwhite thorn,
  On nature's mossy pillow ;
A' round my seat the flowers were strewed,
That frae the wild wood I had pu'd,
To weave mysel' a summer snood,
  To pleasure my dear fellow.

I twined the woodbine round the rose,
  Its richer hues to mellow,
Green sprigs of fragrant birk I chose,
  To busk the sedge sae yellow.
The crawflower blue, and meadow-pink,
I wove in primrose-braided link ;
But little, little did I think
  I should have wove the willow.

My bonnie lad was forced afar,
  Tossed on the raging billow ;
Perhaps he's fa'n in bluidy war,
  Or wrecked on rocky shallow :
Yet, aye I hope for his return,
As round our wonted haunts I mourn,
And often by the woodland burn,
  I pu' the weeping willow.

O Lassie, will you tak' a man?

Air—" Whistle o'er the lave o't."

O LASSIE, will you tak' a man,
Rich in house, and gear, and lan'?
De'il tak' the cash that I should ban,
  Nae mair I'll be the slave o't.

I'll buy you claise to busk you braw,
A riding pony, pad and a';
On fashion's tap we'll drive awa',
    Whip, spur, and a' the lave o't.

Oh, poortith is a wintry day!
Cheerless, blirtie, cauld, and blac,
But basking under fortune's ray,
    There's joy whate'er ye'd have o't.

Then gie's your han' ye'll be my wife,
I'll mak' you happy a' your life;
We'll row in love and siller rife,
    Till death wind up the lave o't.

I'll Love my dear Jeanie.

Air—"My laddie is gane."

From the rude bustling camp to the calm rural plain,
I'm come, my dear Jeanie, to bless thee again;
Still burning for honour our warriors may roam,
But the laurel I wished for, I've won it at home:
All the glories of conquest no joy could impart,
When far from the kind little girl of my heart;
Now, safely returned, I will leave thee no more,
But love my dear Jeanie till life's latest hour.

The sweets of retirement, how pleasing to me!
Possessing all worth, my dear Jeanie, in thee!
Our flocks early bleating will make us to joy,
And our raptures exceed the warm tints in the sky;
In sweet rural pastines our days still will glide,
Till time looking back will admire at his speed,
Still blooming in virtue, though youth then be o'er,
I'll love my dear Jeanie till life's latest hour.

All hail! Ye dear Romantic Scenes.

All hail! ye dear romantic scenes,
    Where aft, as eve stole o'er the sky,
Ye've found me by the mountain streams,
    Where blooming wild-flowers charm the eye.

The sun's now setting in the west—
　Mild are his beams on hill and plain;
No sound is heard save Killoch burn,
　Deep murmuring down its woody glen.

Green be thy banks, thou silver stream
　That winds the flowery braes among,
Where aft I've woo'd the Scottish muse,
　And raptur'd wove the rustic song.

Ye Wooer Lads wha Greet and Grane.

Air—"Callum Brogach."

YE wooer lads wha greet and grane,
Wha preach and fleech and mak' a mane,
An' pine yoursel's to skin and bane,
　Come a' to Callum Brogach.
I'll learn you here the only art
To win a bonnie lassie's heart;
Just tip wi' gowd Love's siller dart
　Like dainty Callum Brogach.

I ca'd her aye my sonsie doo,
The fairest flower that e'er I knew;
Yet, like a souple spankie grew,
　She fled frae Callum Brogach.
But soon's she heard the guinea ring,
She turn'd as I had been a king,
Wi'—"Tak' my hand or ony thing,
　Dear, dainty Callum Brogach!"

Its gowd can mak' the blind to see,
Can bring respect where nane wad be,
And Cupid ne'er shall want his fee
　Frae dainty Callum Brogach.
Nae mair wi' greetin' blin' your een,
Nae mair wi' sighin' warm the win',
But hire the gettlin for your frien',
　Like dainty Callum Brogach.

Away, Gloomy Care.

AWAY, gloomy care, there's no place for thee here,
    Where so many good fellows are met,
Thou would'st dun the poor bard ev'ry day in the year,
    Yet I'm sure I am none in thy debt.
Go, soak thy old skin in the miser's small beer,
    And keep watch in his cell all the night;
And if in the morning thou dar'st to appear,
    By Jove, I shall drown thee outright.

The Soldier's Adieu.

THE weary sun's gane doun the west,
    The birds sit noddin' on the tree,
All nature now inclines for rest,
    But rest there's none allowed for me :
The trumpet calls to war's alarms,
    The rattling drum forbids my stay;
Ah! Nancy, bless thy soldier's arms,
    Ere morn I shall be far away.

Oh! Weep not, my Love.

OH! weep not, my love, though I go to the war,
    For soon I'll return with honours to thee;   .
The soul-rising pibroch is sounding afar,
    And the clans are assembling in Morar-craiglee :
Our flocks are all plunder'd, our herdsmen are murder'd,
    And, fir'd with oppression, aveng'd we shall be;
To-morrow we'll vanquish those ravaging English,
    And then I'll return to thy baby and thee.

Sing on, thou sweet warbler.

SING on, thou sweet warbler, thy glad e'ening song,
And charm the lone echoes the green woods among;
As dear unto thee is the sun's setting beam,
So dear unto me is the soul's melting dream :
The dark winter frowning, all pleasure disowning,
Shall strip thy green woods and be deaf to thy moaning;
But dark stormy winter is yet far away,
Then let us be glad when all nature is gay.

Lone in yon dark sequestr'd Grove.

LONE in yon dark sequester'd grove,
   Poor hapless Lubin strays,
A prey to ill-requited love,
   He spends his joyless days.
Ah, cruel Jessie! couldst thou know
   What worthy heart was thine,
Thou ne'er hadst wrong'd poor Lubin so,
   Nor left that heart to pine.

Two Original Songs.

I.

THE evening sun's gaen down the west,
   The birds sit noddin' on the tree;
All nature now prepares for rest,
   But rest prepared there's none for me.
The trumpet sounds to war's alarms,
   The drums they beat, the fife's they play,—
Come, Mary, cheer me wi' thy charms,
   For the morn I will be far away.

     Good night and joy, good night and joy,
      Good night and joy be wi' you a';
     For since it's so that I must go,
      Good night and joy be wi' you a'!

I grieve to leave my comrades dear,
   I mourn to leave my native shore,—
To leave my aged parents here,
   And the bonnie lass whom I adore.
But tender thoughts maun now be hush'd,
   When danger calls I must obey,—
The transport waits us on the coast,
   And the morn I will be far away.
     Good night and joy, &c.

Adieu, dear Scotia's sea-beat coast!
   Though bleak and drear thy mountains be,
When on the heaving ocean tost,
   I'll cast a wishful look to thee!

And now, dear Mary, fare thee well!
May Providence thy guardian be!
Or in the camp, or on the field,
    I'll heave a sigh, and think on thee!
    Good night and joy, &c.

II.

WHEN I the dreary mountains pass'd,
    My ain kind dearie, O,
I thought on thee, my bonnie lass,
    Although I wasna near thee, O.
My heart within me was right sad,
    When others they were cheerie, O,
They little kent I thought on thee,
    My ain kind dearie, O!

But now an I ha'e won till Ayr,
    Although I'm gae an' wearie, O,
I'll tak' a glass into my han',
    An drink to you, my dearie, O.
Cheer up your heart, my bonnie lass,
    And see you dinna wearie, O;
In twice three ooks, gin I be spared,
    I'se come again, and see thee, O.

    And row thee up, and row thee down,
        And row thee till I wearie, O,
    And row thee o'er the lea rig,
        My ain kind dearie, O!

Dirge.

Written on reading an account of Robert Burns' funeral.

LET grief for ever cloud the day,
That saw our Bard borne to the clay;
Let joy be banished every eye,
And nature, weeping, seem to cry—

    "He's gone, he's gone! he's frae us torn!
    The ae best fellow e'er was born."

Let Sol resign his wonted powers,
Let chilling north winds blast the flowers ;
That each may drop its withering head,
And seem to mourn our Poet dead.
    " He's gone, he's gone !" &c.

Let shepherds, from the mountain's steep,
Look down on widow'd Nith, and weep ;
Let rustic swains their labours leave,
And sighing, murmur o'er his grave—
    " He's gone, he's gone !" &c.

Let bonny Doon and winding Ayr
Their bushy banks in anguish tear,
While many a tributary stream,
Pours down its griefs to swell the theme—
    " He's gone, he's gone !" &c.

All dismal let the night descend,
Let whirling storms the forests rend,
Let furious tempests sweep the sky,
And dreary howling caverns cry—

    " He's gone, he's gone ! he's frae us torn !
    The ae best fellow e'er was born."

TANNAHILL'S POEMS.

The Soldier's Return.

PERSONS REPRESENTED.

THE LAIRD, *colonel of a Scots Regiment.*
GAFFER, *the laird's tenant.*
MUIRLAND WILLIE, *an old rich dotard.*
HARRY, *in love with Jean.*
MIRREN, *Gaffer's wife—a foolish old woman.*
JEAN, *daughter of Gaffer and Mirren, beloved by Muirland, but in love
    with Harry.*

ACT I.—SCENE I.

A range of hills, o'erhung wi' waving woods,
That spread their dark green bosoms to the clouds,
And seem to crave the tribute of a shower,
Grateful to woodland plant and mountain flower:
A glen beneath, frae whilk a bickering burn
Strayes round the knowes, wi' bonnie wimpling turn,
Syne trotting downwards through the cultur'd lauds,
Runs by where Gaffer's humble biggin stands;
His wife and him are at some family plea,
To hear what ails them, just step in and see.

GAFFER *and* MIRREN.

Mirren. Love should be free! my trouth, but ye craw
You a guidman and canna rule your house!   [crouse,
Had I a father's power, I'd let her see
Wi' vengeance, whether or no that love be free.
She kens right weel Muirland has ilk thing ready,
And's fit to keep her busked like a lady;

F

Yet soon's she hears me mention Muirland Willie,
She skits and flings like ony towmont filly.
De'il nor ye'd broke your leg, gaun cross the hallan,
That day ye fee'd the skelpor Highland callan;
We've fed him, clad him, what's our mense for't a' ?
Base wretch, to steal our daughter's heart awa' !
Love should be free ! guid trouth, a bonnie story !
That Muirland maun be lost for Highland Harry.
Muirland comes down this night—to talk's nae use,
For she shall gi'e consent or lea' the house.
Odsaffs ! my heart did never wallop cadger,
Than when the laird took Harry for a sodger ;
And now she sits a' day, sae douff and blearie,
And sings love sangs about her Highland Harry.

Gaf. Indeed, guidwife, the lad did weel enough,
Was eydent aye, and deftly held the plough ;
But Muirland's up in years, and shame to tell,
Has ne'er been married, though as auld's mysel' ;
His locks are lyart, and his joints are stiff,
A staff wad set him better than a wife.
Sooner shall roses in December blaw,
Sooner shall tulips flourish i' the snaw,
Sooner the woods shall bud wi' winter's cauld,
Than lasses quit a young man for an auld :
Yet, she may tak' him gin she likes for me,
My say shall never mak' them disagree.

Mir. Ye hinna the ambition o' a' mouse ;
She'll gie consent this night, or lea' the house.

Enter JEAN, *in haste.*

Jean. Father, the sheep are nibblin' i' the corn,
Wee Sandy's chained auld Bawtie to the thorn,
And bawsen'd Crummock's broken frae the sta' ;
Oh ! a's gane wrang since Harry gaed awa'.

Gaf. A house divided, a' gangs to the devil. [*Aside, exit.*

Mir. Daughter, come here ! now, let us reason civil,
Isn't siller mak's our ladies gang so braw ?
Isn't siller buys their cloaks and bonnets a' ?
Isn't siller busks them up wi' silks and satins,
Wi' umbrella, muffs, claith shoon, and pattons ?
Our lady, what is't gars us courtesy till her,

And ca' her ma'am ? why, just 'cause she has siller :
Isn't siller mak's our gentles fair and sappy ?
Whilk lets us see, it's siller mak's folk happy.

    Jean. Mither, ae simple question let me spier,
Is Muirland fat or fair wi' a' his gear ?
Auld croighlin' wight, to hide the ills o' age,
He capers like a monkey on a stage ;
And cracks, and sings, and giggles sae light and kittle,
Wi' his auld beard slaver'd wi' tobacco spittle.

    Mir. Peace, wardless slut ! oh, when will youth be wise !
Ye'll slight your carefu' mither's guid advice ;
I've brought you up, and made you what ye are,
And that's your thanks for a' my toil and care.
Muirland comes down this night, sae drap your stodgin,
For ye must gi'e consent, or change your lodgin'. [*Exit.*

    Jean. E'en turn me out, Muirland I'll never marry :
What's wealth or life without my dearest Harry ?

SONG.

Our bonnie Scots lads in their green tartan plaids,
    Their blue-belted bonnets, and feathers sae braw,
Ranked up on the green were fair to be seen,
    But my bonnie young laddie was fairest of a' ;
His cheeks were as red as the sweet heather bell,
    Or the red western cloud looking down on the snaw ;
His lang yellow hair o'er his braid shoulders fell,
    And the e'en o' the lassies were fix'd on him a'.

My heart sunk wi' wae on the wearifu' day,
    When torn frae my bosom, they march'd him awa' ;
He bade me farewell, he cried, " Oh, be leal ! "
    And his red cheeks were wet wi' the tears that did fa'.
Ah ! Harry, my love, though thou ne'er shouldst return,
    Till life's latest hour I thy absence will mourn ;
And mem'ry shall fade like a leaf on the tree,
    Ere my heart spare ae thought on anither but thee.

SCENE II.

Harry returned, as servant to the laird,
Finds, for a while, his presence may be spared,
And here, his lane, he wanders o'er each scene,
Where first he loved, and fondly woo'd his **Jean :**
He sees her cot, and fain would enter in,
But weel he minds her mither's no his frien'.

    Harry. Tir'd with the painful sight of **human ills,**
Hail, Caledonia ! hail, my native hills !

Here exil'd virtue rears her humble cell,
With nature's jocund, honest sons to dwell;
And hospitality, with open door,
Invites the stranger and the wand'ring poor:
Though winter scowls along our northern sky,
In hardships rear'd we learn humanity;
Nor dare deceit here point her rankling dart,
A Scotchman's eye's the window of his heart.
   When fate and adverse fortune bore me far,
O'er field and flood, to join the din of war,
My young heart sicken'd, gloomy was my mind,
My love, my friends, my country, all behind:
But whether toss'd upon the briny flood,
Or dragg'd to combat in the scene of blood,
Hope, like an angel, charm'd my cares away,
And pointed forward to this happy day.
Full well I mind yon breckan-skirted thorn,
That sheds its milk-white blossoms by the burn;
There first my heart life's highest bliss did prove—
'Twas there my Jeanie, blushing, own'd her love.
Yon dark green plantings on the mountain's brow,
Yon yellow whins and broomy knowes below,
Bring to my mind the happy, happy days,
I spent with her upon these rural braes;
But while remembrance thus my bosom warms,
I long to clasp my charmer in my arms.　　　　[*Exit.*

SCENE III.

Now Mirren's to the burn to sine her kirn,
Here Jeanie waefu' sits and reels her pirn,
While honest Gaffer, aye for peace inclined,
Is haflins vex'd, and freely speaks his mind.

Gaffer. Thy mither's gair, and set upon the war',
It's Muirland's gear that gars her like the carl,
But nature bids thee spurn the silly tike,
And wha would wed wi' ane they canna like?
Just speak thy mind, and tell him, ance for a',
That eighteen ne'er can 'gree wi' sixty-twa;
A mair disgusting sight I never knew,
Than youthfu' folly 'neath an auld gray pow.

Enter MIRREN, *blythely.*

Mir. Here comes our neebour, hurrying frae the muir,
Mak' a' things snod—fy! haste, red up the floor;
The like o' him to visit you and me
Reflects an honour on our family;
Now, lassie, mind my high command is this,
Whatever Muirland says, ye'll answer yes.
    Jean. Whatever Muirland says, it shall be so,
But soon as morning comes, I'll answer, no!   [*Aside.*

Enter MUIRLAND.

Muir. Peace to the biggin', he, he, he! how's a'?
    Mir. Gaily, I thank you—William, come awa'.
And tell us how ye fen' this night yoursel'?
    Muir. He, he! His name be prais'd, faith, unco weel,
I ne'er was half sae strang in a' my days;
I'm grown sae fat, I'm like to burst my claes!
Nae wonder o't, I'm just now at my prime:
I'm just now five and thretty come the time!
Ho, ho, ho, ho! I pity them wha're auld,
Yestreen I catch'd a wee bit croighle o' cauld.
    Gaf. I might excuse a foolish, untaught bairn,
But second childhood, sure, will never learn.   [*Aside, exit.*

[MUIRLAND, *half blind with age, slips on his spectacles
    secretly, recognizes* JEAN, *advances to her and sings.*]

SONG.

Tune—"Whistle o'er the lave o't."

Oh, lassie, will you tak' a man,
Rich in house, and gear, and lan';
De'il tak' the cash that I should ban,
    Nae mair I'll be the slave o't.

I'll buy you claes to busk you braw,
A riding pony, pad, and a';
On fashion's tap we'll drive awa',
    Whip, spur, and a' the lave o't.

Oh, poortith is a wintry day,
Cheerless, blirtie, cauld, and blae;
But basking under fortune's ray,
    There's joy whate'er ye'd have o't.

Then gie's your han' ye'll be my wife,
I'll mak' you happy a' your life;
We'll row in love and siller rife,
    Till death wind up the lave o't.

Mir. Nae toiling then to raise a heavy rent;
Our fortune's made—oh, lassie, gi'e consent.

[Aside to Jean.

Muir. Ye'll get a gouden ring and siller brooch,
And now and then we'll hurl in a coach:
To shaw we're gentle, when we walk on fit,
In passing puir folks, how we'll flucht and skit!

Jean. And tho' ye're rather auld, I'm rather young;
Our ages mixed will stop the warld's tongue.

Muir. Auld, said ye? no! ye surely speak in jest,
Your mither kens I'm just now at my best!

Mir. The lass is blunt; she means na as she says:
Ye ne'er looked half sae weel in a' your days!
Wi' canny care I've spun a pickle yarn,
That honest-like we may set aff our bairn;
If gang wi' me, we'll o'er to Wabster Pate's,
And see him weaving at the bridal sheets.

Muir. The bridal sheets! he, he, he, he, what bliss!
The bridal sheets! oh, gi'e's an erl-kiss.

Mir. Fy! come awa', and dinna think o' kissing
Till ance Mess John ha'e gi'en you baith his blessing.

[Exit.

JEAN, *solus.*

Alas! my mither's just like Whang the miller,
O'erturns her house in hopes o' finding siller;
For soon's I see the morning's first faint gleam,
She wakens sorrowing frae her gouden dream.

SONG.

Tune—" Morneen I gaberland."

Blythe was the time when he fee'd wi' my father, O,
Happy were the days when we herded thegither, O,
Sweet were the hours when he rowed me in his plaidie, O,
And vowed to be mine, my dear Highland laddie, O.
But ah! waes me! wi' their sodgering sae gaudy, O,
The laird's wysed awa' my braw Highland laddie, O;
Misty are the glens, and the dark hills sae cloudy, O,
That aye seemed sae blythe wi' my dear Highland laddie, O.

The blaeberry banks, now, are lonesome and dreary, O,
Muddy are the streams that gushed down sae clearly, O,
Silent are the rocks that echoed sae gladly, O,
The wild melting strains of my dear Highland laddie, O

Farewell, my ewes! and farewell, my doggie, O,
Farewell, ye knowes! now sae cheerless and scroggie, O,
Farewell, Glenfeoch! my mammie and my daddie, O,
I will lea' you a' for my dear Highland laddie, O.

Through distant towns I'll stray a hapless stranger,
In thoughts of him I'll brave pale want and danger;
And as I go, poor, weeping, mournfu' ponderer,
Still some kind heart will cheer the weary wanderer.

[*Exit.*

———

ACT II.—SCENE I. GAFFER'S HOUSE.

JEAN, *solus.*

Lang syne, beside the woodland burn,
   Amang the broom sae yellow,
I leaned me 'neath the milkwhite thorn,
   On nature's mossy pillow;
A' round my seat the flowers were strewed,
That frae the wild wood I had pu'd,
To weave mysel' a summer snood,
   To pleasure my dear fellow.

I twined the woodbine round the rose,
   It's richer hue to mellow;
Green sprigs of fragrant birk I chose,
   To busk the sedge sae yellow.
The crow-flower blue, and meadow-pink,
I wove in primrose-braided link;
But little, little did I think
   I should have wove the willow.

My bonnie lad was forced afar,
   Tossed on the raging billow;
Perhaps he's fa'n in bluidy war,
   Or wrecked on rocky shallow:
Yet, aye I hope for his return,
As round our wonted haunts I mourn,
And often by the woodland burn,
   I pu' the weeping willow.

Enter MUIRLAND.

Muir. Faith! Patie's spool jinks through wi' wondrous
   might,
And aye it minds me o' the bridal night.
I've rough o' sheets, sae never fash your thumb:
Oh, gi'e's a kiss afore your minnie come!

Harry enters—Jeanie kens him ;
First he grips her to his breast ;
Willie gapes, and glowers, and sanes him,
Rins and roars like ane possessed.
Wild wilyart fancies revel in his brain :
They baith run aff and lea' him a' his lane.

Muir. Oh, murder, murder ! oh, I'll die wi' fear :
Oh, Gaffer, Mirren ! oh, come here, come here !

Enter MIRREN, *in haste.*

Mir. The pewet's screighin' owre the spankie-cairn :
My heart bodes ill, oh, William, where's my bairn ?
Muir. A great red dragon, wi' a warlock claw,
Has come, and wi' your daughter flown awa' !

Enter. GAFFER, *in haste.*

Gaf. What awfu' cry was yon I heard within ?
What mak's you glower, and what caused a' yon din ?
Mir. A great big dragon, wi' a red airn claw,
Has come, and wi' your daughter flown awa' !

[*Crying*

Muir. Its head was covered wi' a black airn ladle ;
It had black legs, and tail as sharp's a needle :
A great red e'e stood starin' in its breast ;
I'm like to swarf—oh ! 'twas a fearfu' beast.
Mir. The craw that bigged in the stackyard thorn,
Screighed and forsook its nest when she was born ;
Three pyats crossed the kirk when she was christened,
I've heard it telled, and trembled while I listened :
Oh, dool and wae, my dream's been read right soon !
Yestreen I dreamed twa mice had holed the moon.
Gaf. The sword o' justice never fa's unwrought for !
But come, alive or dead, let's seek our daughter.
Muir. I'll no be weel this month, oh, what a fright !
I'll no gang owre the muir my lane this night.

[*Exit.*

SCENE II.

A briery bank, ahint a broomy knowe,
Our youthfu' loving couple, hid frae view,
Their vows renew, and here wi' looks sae sweet,
They set their tryst where neist again to meet.

Jean. My heart shall, ever gratefu', bless the laird,
Wha showed my dearest Harry such regard ;

Restored you to our hills and rural plain,
Frae war's fatigues, safe to my arms again.

Harry. Remote from bustling camps and war's alarms,
Thus, let me ever clasp thee in my arms.

Jean. But here, my lad, we darena weel be seen ;
Dear Harry ! say, where will we meet at e'en ?

HARRY'S SONG.

We'll meet beside the dusky glen, on yon burn side,
Where the bushes form a cozy den, on yon burn side;
Though the broomy knowes be green, yet, there we may be seen,
But we'll meet, we'll meet at e'en, down by yon burn side.

I'll lead thee to the birken bower, on yon burn side ;
Sae sweetly wove wi' woodbine flower, on yon burn side ;
There the busy prying eye ne'er disturbs the lovers' joy,
While in ither's arms they lie, down by yon burn side.

Awa', ye rude unfeeling crew, frae yon burn side,
Those fairy scenes are no for you, by yon burn side ;
There fancy smoothes her theme, by the sweetly murmuring stream,
And the rock-lodged echoes skim, down by yon burn side.

Now the planting taps are tinged wi' goud on yon burn side,
And gloamin' draws her foggy shroud o'er yon burn side,
Far frae the noisy scene, I'll through the fields alane,
There we'll meet, my ain dear Jean ! down by yon burn side.

Jean. I'll jeer my ancient wooer hame, and then
I'll meet you at the opening o' the glen.

[*Exit separately.*

SCENE III.—GAFFER'S HOUSE.

With unsuccessfu' search the ghost-rid three,
Ha'e sought the boortree bank, and hemlock lea,
The nettle-corner, and the rowan-tree brae—
Sae here they come, a' sunk in deepest wae,

Gaf. Alas ! guidwife our search has been in vain,
Come o't what will, my bosom's wrung wi' pain ;
I haflins think his een ha'e him mislipened,
But oh ! it's hard to say what may ha'e happened.

Enter MUIRLAND *running.*

Muir. Preserve's ! oh, haste ye ! rin, mak' mettle heels ;
I saw the dragon spankin' o'er the fields.

[*They stop from going out on seeing Jean enter.*]

Jean. What mak's you stare so strange—what's wrang
        wi' Willie ?
He roars as loud's a horn, though auld and silly.

Muir. I'm no sae auld—my pith ye yet may brag on ;
But, Jeanie, love ! how did you match the dragon ?
   Jean. Auld blethcrin' wight ! the gowk's possessed, I
      ween.
   Gaf. Come, daughter ! clear this riddle—where ha'e ye
      been ?
   Jean. Father, rare news ! our laird's come hame this day ;
His man ca'd in to tell us by the way,
Dressed in his sodger's clothes, wi' scarlet coat :
He is a bonnie lad, fu' weel I wot.
   Muir. The dragon ! he, he, he ! I've been delicred ;
I'll wear a scarlet coat, too, when we're married.
   Gaf. Our laird come hame ! and safe but skaith or scar ;
I'll owre, and hear the history o' the war.
Us country folk are bound like in a cage up ;
I'll owre, and hear about that place ca'd Egypt :
I long to hear him tell a' what he's seen,
For four long winters he awa' has been.
Wife ! fetch my bonnet that I coft last owk ;
Here ! brush my coat—fy, Jean ! tak' off that powk.
   Mir. Toot, snuff ! 'bout news ye needna be sa thrang ;
Let's set the bridal night afore ye gang.
   Muir. The bridal night ! he, he ! he, he ! that's right :
The bridal night ! he, he ! the bridal night.
   Jean. I'll hang as high's the steeple, in a wuddie,
Before I wed wi' that auld kecklin' body.
   Mir. Was mither e'er sae plagued wi' a daughter ?
Oh, that's her thank for a' the length I've brought her !
   Gaf. This racket in a house—it is a shame :   [*Crying.*
I'll thank you, Muirland, to be steppin' hame,
   Jean. Auld swirlen, slaethorn, crumsheugh, crooked
      wight,
Gae wa', and ne'er again come in my sight !
   Muir. That e'er my lugs were doomed to hear sic words,
Whilk rush into my heart like point l swords !
Frae me let younkers warning tak' in time,
And wed, ere dozened down ayont their prime :
Oh, me ! I canna gang ; 'twill break my heart ;
Let's hae a farewell peep afore we part.
[*He puts on his spectacles, stares at Jean, and roars ludi-*
      crously.   Exit crying.]

Enter the LAIRD, *attended by* HARRY.

Laird. Well, how d'ye do, my worthy tenants, pray;
How fares good Gaffer since I went away?
Gaf. My noble laird! thanks to the lucky star
That steered you hame, safe through the storms o' war.
    Laird, Thanks, honest friend! I know your heart of
      truth;
But for my safety, thank this gallant youth:
He saved my life—to him I owe my fame,
And gratitude shall still revere his name.
    Gaf. May heaven's post-angel swift my blessings carry;
He saved your life—preserve me, it is Harry!
Thrice welcome, lad! here, gi'es a shake o' yer paw;
Ye've mended hugely since you gaed awa.'
    Harry. Yes, sodgering brushes up a person's frame,
But at the heart I hope I'm still the same.
    Gaf. Your promise to do weel, I see you've keepen't.
He saved your life—oh, tell me how it happened!
    Laird. 'Twas March the eighth, that memorable day,
Our sea-worn troops, all weary with delay,
For six long days, storm-rocked, we lay off-shore,
And heard the enemy's guns menacing roar.
At length, the wished-for orders came, to land
And drive the foe back from the mounded strand;
Then, each a hero, on the decks we stood,
Launched out our boats, and speeded all we could;
While clouds of sulphureous smoke obscured the view,
And showers of grape-shot from their batteries flew,
A brother captain, seated by my side,
Received a shot—he sank, he quivered, died;
With friendly hand I closed his life-gone-eyes,
Our sighs, our tears, were all his obsequies.
Then, as our rowers strove with lengthened sweep,
Back from the stern I tumbled in the deep,
And sure had perished, for each pressing wave
Seemed emulous to be a soldier's grave,
Had not this gallant youth, at danger's shrine,
Offering his life a sacrifice for mine,
Leaped from the boat, and beat his billowy way
To where I belched and struggled in the sea:

With godlike arm sustained life's sinking hope,
Till the succeeding rowers picked us up.

    Gaf. Fair fa' your worth, my brave young sodger lad !
To see you safe returned my heart is glad :
Ilk cottar round will long your name regard,
And bless you for your kindness to the laird.

    Laird. And when the day's hot work of war was done,
Each fight-tired soldier leaning on his gun,
I sought my brave deliverer and made
An offer with what influence I had,
To raise his fortune—but he shunned reward,
Yet warmly thanked me for my kind regard.
Then, as in warmth I praised his good behaviour,
He modestly besought me this one favour,
That, if surviving when the war was o'er,
And safe returned to Scotia once more,
I'd ask your will for him to wed your daughter :
A manly, virtuous heart he home hath brought her.

    Gaf. With a' my heart he has my free consent ;
Wife, what say ye ? I hope ye're weel content.

    Mir. A mither's word stands neither here nor there :
Tak' him or no, I'm sure I dinna care.

    Laird. Accept this trifle as young Harry's wife ;
                        [Gives his purse to Jean.
Money is no equivalent for life ;
And take this ring—good mistress, here's another !
With this I enlist you for young Harry's mother.

    Jean. Excuse me, sir, my lips can not impart
The warm emotions of my grateful heart.

    Mir. It's goud, it's goud ! oh, yes, sir, I agree ;
Gaffer, it's goud ! yes, love should aye be free.

    Gaf. Daft woman, cease !

    Laird.   And as for you, good Gaffer,
My steward will inform what's in your favour.
Meantime, prepare the wedding to your wills,
Invite my tenants from the neighbouring hills,
Then feast, drink, dance, till each one tynes his senses,
And spare no cost, for I shall pay the expenses.

    Harry. Most generous sir, to tell how much I owe,
I'm weak in words ; let time and actions show.

    Laird. My dearest friend, I pray, no more of this ;
Would I could make you happy as I wish !

From him most benefited most is due,
And sure the debt belongs from me to you :
Attend the mansion soon as morning's light.
And now, my friends, I wish you all good night !　　[*Exit.*

　　Harry. Great is his soul! soft be his bed of rest,
Whose only wish is to make others blessed.
　　Mir. I'll gang to kirk neist Sunday—odd's my life !
This gouden ring will vex Glen Craigie's wife.
　　Gaf. Wife, fy ! let pride and envy gang thegither ;
This house, I hope, will ne'er be fashed wi' either :
Aye be content wi' what ye ha'e yoursel',
And never grudge to see a neighbour's weel.
But Harry, man ! I lang to hear you sing ;
Ye wont to make our glens and plantings ring.
　　Harry. My heart was never on a cantier key,
I'll sing you one with true spontaneous glee.

SONG.

Tune—" My laddie is gane."

From the rude bustling camp to the calm rural plain,
I'm come, my dear Jeanie, to bless thee again ;
Still burning for honour our warriors may roam,
But the laurel I wished for, I've won it at home :
All the glories of conquest no joy could impart,
When far from the kind little girl of my heart ;
Now, safely returned, I will leave thee no more,
But love my dear Jeanie till life's latest hour.

The sweets of retirement, how pleasing to me !
Possessing all worth, my dear Jeanie, in thee !
Our flocks early bleating will make us to joy,
And our raptures exceed the warm tints to the sky ;
In sweet rural pastimes our days still will glide,
Till time looking back will admire at his speed,
Still blooming in virtue, though youth then be o'er,
I'll love my dear Jeanie till life's latest hour.

Enter MUIRLAND.

　　Muir. That's nobly sung, my hearty sodger callan,
I've heard you a' ahint the byre-door hallan ;
I see my faults, I've changed my foolish views,
And now I'm come to beg for your excuse :
The sang sings true, I own't without a swither,
" Auld age and young can never 'gree thegither."
I think, through life I'll mak' a canny fen',
Wi' hurcheon Nancy o' the hazel glen ;

She has my vows, but aye I let her stand,
In hopes to win that bonnie lassie's hand;
Oh! foolish thought, I maist could greet wi' spite,
But it was sleeky love had a' the wyte;
Nae mair let fortune pride in her deserts,
Her goud can purchase hands, but ne'er can sowther hearts.

Gaf. The man wha sees his faults and strives to men' 'em,
Does mair for virtue than he ne'er had haen 'em;
And he wha deals in scandal only gains
A rich repay of scandal for his pains.
Ye ha'e our free excuse, ye needna doubt it,
Ye'll ne'er frae us mair hear a word about it.

Muir. That's a' I wish'd—I couldna bide the thought,
To live on earth, and bear your scorn in aught;
My heart's now whole—ye soon shall hear the banns
Proclaim'd i' the parish kirk 'tween me and Nanse.
I'm no the first auld chiel wha's gotten a slight;
I'll owre the muir—sae fareweel a' this night.   [*Exit.*

Gaf. Of a' experience, that bears aff the bell,
Whilk lets a body rightly ken himsel'.

Jean. May lasses, when their joes are far frae hame,
Bid straggling wooers gang the gates they came;
Else, aiblins, when their moonshine course shifts past,
They'll ha'e to wed auld dotards at the last.

Mir. Guidwives should aye be subject to their men;
I'll ne'er speak contrar to your will again.

Gaf. That's right, guidwife, I'm sure I weel may say,
Glenfeoch never saw sae bless'd a day.
Young folks, we'll set the bridal day the morn:
But, lucky, haste! bring ben the Christmas horn;
Let's pour ae sacred bumper to the laird,
A glass, to crown a wish, was never better wair'd.

Harry. While I was yet a boy, my parents died,
And left me poor and friendless, waud'ring wide;
Your goodness found me—'neath your fostering care,
I learn'd those precepts which I'll still revere:
And now, to Heaven for length of life I pray,
With filial love your goodness to repay.

Gaf. This sacred maxim let us still regard,
That virtue ever is its own reward;
And what we give to succour the distress'd,
Calls down from Heaven a blessing on the rest.

Lines.

RICH Gripus pretends he's my patron and friend,
That all times to serve me he's willing;
But he looks down so sour on the suppliant poor,
That I'd starve ere I'd ask him one shilling.

The promotion.

WHEN the devil got notice old Charon was dead,
He wished for some blockhead to row in his stead;
For he feared one with intellect discoveries might make,
Of his tortures and racks t'other side of the lake;
So for true native dullness and want of discernment,
He sought the whole world, and gave John the preferment.

On a man of character.

WEE A———, self-sainted wight,
    If e'er he win to heaven,
The veriest wretch, though black as pitch,
    May rest he'll be forgiven.
Wi' holy pride he cocks his nose,
    And talks o' honest dealings;
But when our webs are at the close,
    He nips off twa three shillings.

Antipathy.

I SCORN the selfish, purse-proud b——
Who piques himself on being rich
With two-score pounds, late legacied,
Saved by his half-starved father's greed.
To former neighbours not one word;
He bows obsequious to my lord.
In public, see him! how he capers!
Looks big, steps short, pulls out his papers;
And from a silly, puppish dance,
Commences the great man at once.

To a Person

NOTED FOR HIS ASSUMED SANCTITY.

WHAT need'st thou dread the end of sin,
  The dire reward of evil :
Keep but that black infernal grin,
  'Twill scar the very devil.

Lines to Wl. M'Laren,

TO ATTEND A MEETING OF THE "BURNS' ANNIVERSARY SOCIETY."

KING GEORDIE issues out his summons,
To ca' his bairns, the lairds and commons,
To creesh the nation's mooly heels,
And butter commerce rusty wheels,
And see what new, what untried tax,
Will lie the easiest on our backs.
  The priest convenes his scandal-court,
To ken what houghmigandie sport
Has been gaun on within the parish,
Since last they met, their funds to cherish.
  But I, the servant of Apollo,
Whose mandates I am proud to follow ;
He bids me warn you, as the friend
Of Burns's fame, that ye'll attend,
Neist Friday's e'en, in Lucky Wright's,
To spend the best, the wale o' nights.
Sae, under pain o' half a mark,
Ye'll come, as signed by me, the clerk.
                    ROBERT TANNAHILL.

Will MacNeil's Elegy.

"He was a man without a clag;
  His heart was frank without a flaw."

RESPONSIVE to the roaring floods,
Ye winds, howl plaintive through the woods;
Thou gloomy sky, pour down hail clouds,
                    His death to wail;
For bright as heaven's brightest studs
                    Shin'd Will MacNeil.

He every selfish thought did scorn,
His warm heart in his looks did burn,
Ilk body own'd his kindly turn,
        And gait sac leal ;
A kinder saul was never born
        Than Will MacNeil.

He ne'er kept up a hidlin plack
To spend ahint a comrade's back,
But on the table gar'd it whack
        Wi' free gude will :
Free as the wind on winter stack
        Was Will MacNeil.

He ne'er could bide a narrow saul,
To a' the social virtues caul';
He wish'd ilk sic a fiery scaul',
        His shins to peel :
Nane sic durst herd in field or faul'
        Wi' Will MacNeil.

He aye abhorr'd the spaniel art ;
Aye when he spak' 'twas frae the heart ;
An honest, open, manly part
        He aye uphel' :
" Guile should be davel'd i' the dirt,"
        Said Will MacNeil.

He ne'er had greed to gather gear,
Yet rigid kept his credit clear ;
He ever was to Misery dear,
        Her loss she'll feel :
She aye got saxpence, or a tear,
        Frae Will MacNeil.

In Scotch antiquities he pridet ;
Auld Hardyknute, he kent wha made it ;
The bagpipe too, he sometimes sey'd it ;
        Pibroch and reel .
Our ain auld language few could read it
        Like Will MacNeil.

In wilyart glens he lik'd to stray,
By foggie rocks, or castle gray;
Yet ghaist-red rustics ne'er did say,
                    "Uncanny chiel!"
They filled their horns wi' usquebae
                    To Will MacNeil.

He sail'd and trampet mony a mile,
To visit auld I-columb-kill;
He clamb the heights o' Jura's isle,
                    Wi' weary spiel;
But siccan sights aye pay'd the toil
                    Wi' Will MacNeil.

He rang'd through Morven's hills and glens,
Saw some o' Ossian's moss-grown stanes,
Where rest his low-laid heroes' banes,
                    Deep in the hill;
He croon'd a c'ronach to their names,—
                    Kind Will MacNeil!

He was deep-read in nature's buik,
Explor'd ilk dark mysterious cruik,
Kend a' her laws wi' antrin luik,
                    And that right weel;
But (fate o' genius) death soon tuik
                    Aff Will MacNeil.

Of ilka rock he kent the ore,
He kend the virtues o' ilk flow'r,
Ilk banefu' plant he kent its power,
                    And warn'd frae ill:
A' nature's warks few could explore
                    Like Will MacNeil.

He kend a' creatures, clute and tail
Down frae the lion to the snail,
Up frae the mennoun to the whale,
                    And kraken eel:
Scarce ane could tell their gaits sae weel
                    As Will MacNeil

Nor past he ought thing slightly by,
But with keen scrutinizing eye,
He to its inmaist bore would pry,
　　　　　Wi' wondrous skill;
And teaching ithers aye ga'e joy
　　　　　To Will MacNeil.

He kend auld Archimedes' gait,
What way he burnt the Roman fleet,
"Twas by the rays' reflected heat
　　　　　"Frae speculum steel,
"For bare refraction ne'er could do't,"
　　　　　Said Will MacNeil.

Yet fame his praise did never rair it,
For poortith's weeds obscur'd his merit,
Forby, he had a bashfu' spirit,
　　　　　That sham'd to tell
His worth or wants; let envy spare it,
　　　　　To Will MacNeil.

O Barra, thou wast sair to blame!
I here record it to thy shame,
Thou luit the brightest o' thy name,
　　　　　Unheeded steal,
Through murky life to his lang hame,—
　　　　　Poor Will MacNeil.

He ne'er did wrang to living creature,
For ill, Will hadna't in his nature;
A warm, kind heart his leading feature,
　　　　　His mainspring wheel;
Ilk virtue grew to noble stature
　　　　　In Will MacNeil.

There's no a man that ever ken'd him,
But wi' his tears will lang lament him;
He has na' left his match ahint him,
　　　　　At hame or fiel';
His worth lang on our minds will print him,—
　　　　　Kind Will MacNeil.

But close, my sang; my hameward lays
Are far unfit to speak his praise;
Our happy nights, our happy days,
          Fareweel, fareweel!
Now dowie, mute—tears speak our waes
          For Will MacNeil.

THE CONTRARY.

Get up, my Muse, and sound thy chanter,
Nor langer wi' our feelings saunter;
Ilk true-blue Scot, get up and canter,
          He's hale and weel!
And lang may Fate keep off mischanter
          Frae Will MacNeil.

The Filial Vow.

WHY heaves my mother oft the deep-drawn sigh
Why starts the big tear glistening in her eye?
Why oft retire to hide her bursting grief?
Why seeks she not, nor seems to wish relief?
'Tis for my father, mould'ring with the dead,
My brother, in bold manhood, lowly laid,
And for the pains which age is doom'd to bear,
She heaves the deep-drawn sigh, and drops the secret tear.
Yes, partly these her gloomy thoughts employ,
But mostly this o'erclouds her earthly joy;
She grieves to think she may be burdensome,
Now feeble, old, and tott'ring to the tomb.

Oh hear me, Heaven! and record my vow;
Its non-performance let thy wrath pursue!
I swear—Of what thy providence may give,
My mother shall her due maintenance have.
'Twas hers to guide me through life's early day,
To point out virtue's paths, and lead the way:
Now, while her powers in frigid languor sleep,
'Tis mine to hand her down life's rugged steep,
With all her little weaknesses to bear,
Attentive, kind, to soothe her every care.
'Tis nature bids, and truest pleasure flows
From lessening an aged parent's woes.

Eild:

A FRAGMENT.

THE rough hail rattles through the trees,
 The sullen lift low'rs gloomy gray,
The traveller sees the swelling storm,
 And seeks the ale-house by the way.

But, waes me! for yon widowed wretch,
 Borne down with years and heavy care,
Her sapless fingers scarce can nip
 The wither'd twigs to beet her fire.

Thus youth and vigour fends itsel',
 Its help, reciprocal, is sure;
While dowless Eild, in poortith cauld,
 Is lonely left to stand the stoure.

Stanzas.

WRITTEN WITH A PENCIL ON THE GRAVESTONE OF A DEPARTED FRIEND.

STOP, passenger—here muse awhile—
 Think on his darksome lone abode,
Who late, like thee, did jocund smile,
 But now lies 'neath this cold green sod.

Art thou to vicious ways inclin'd,
 Pursuing pleasure's flow'ry road?
Know—fell Remorse shall rack thy mind,
 When tott'ring to thy cold green sod.

If thou a friend to virtue art,
 Oft pitying burden'd mis'ry's load;
Like thee he had a feeling heart,
 Who lies beneath this cold green sod.

With studious philosophic eye,
 He look'd through nature up to God;
His future hope his greatest joy,
 Who lies beneath this cold green sod.

Go, passenger—revere this truth;
 A life well spent in doing good,
Soothes joyless age, and sprightly youth,
 When drooping o'er the cold green sod.

On Alexander Wilson's Emigration to America.

O DEATH! it's no thy deeds I mourn,
Though oft my heart strings thou hast torn;
'Tis worth and merit left forlorn,
                    Life's ills to dree,
Gars now the pearly, brackish burn
                    Gush frae my e'e.

Is there who feels the melting glow
Of sympathy for ither's wo?
Come let our tears thegither flow;
                    Oh join my mane!
For Wilson, worthiest of us a',
                    For aye is gane.

He bravely strove 'gainst fortune's stream,
While hope held forth a distant gleam;
Till dash'd and dash'd, time after time,
                    On life's rough sea,
He wept his native thankless clime,
                    And sailed away.

The patriot bauld, the social brither,
In him were sweetly joined thegither;
He knaves reprov'd without a swither,
                    In keenest satire,
And taught what mankind owe each ither
                    As sons of nature.

If thou hast heard his wee bit wren
Wail forth its sorrows through the glen,
Tell how his warm, descriptive pen
                    Has thrilled thy saul:
His sensibility sae keen,
                    He felt for all.

Since now he's gane, and Burns is dead,
Ah! wha will tune the Scottish reed?
Her thistle, dowie, hangs its head;
                    Her harp's unstrung
While mountain, river, loch and mead,
                    Remain unsung.

Fareweel, thou much neglected bard !
These lines will speak my warm regard,
While strangers on a foreign sward
     Thy worth hold dear ;
Still some kind heart thy name shall guard
     Unsullied here,

Sonnet to Sincerity.

PURE emanation of the honest soul,
  Dear to my heart, manly Sincerity !
Dissimulation shrinks, a coward foul,
  Before thy noble art-detesting eye.

Thou scorn'st the wretch who acts a double part,
  Obsequious, servile, flattering to betray ;
With smiling face that veils a ranc'rous heart,
  Like sunny morning of tempestuous day.

Thou spurnest the sophist, with his guilty lore,
  Whom int'rest prompts to weave the specious snare ;
In independence rich, thou own'st a store
  Of conscious worth, which changelings never share.

Then come, bright virtue, with thy dauntless brow,
  And crush deceit, vile monster, reptile-low.

Lines

WRITTEN ON READING THE " PLEASURES OF HOPE."

How seldom 'tis the Poet's happy lot
T' inspire his readers with the fire he wrote ;
To strike those chords that wake the latent thrill,
And wind the willing passions to his will :
Yes, Campbell, sure that happy lot is thine,
With fit expression, rich from Nature's mine,
Like old Timotheus, skilful plac'd on high,
To rouse revenge, or soothe to sympathy.
Blest Bard ! who chose no paltry local theme,—
Kind hope through wide creation is the same ;
Yes, Afric's sons shall one day burst their chains,
Will read thy lines, and bless thee for thy pains ;

Fame yet shall waft thy name to India's shore,
Where next to Brahma they thee will adore ;
And hist'ry's page, exulting in thy praise,
Will proudly hand thee down to future days—
Detraction foil'd reluctant quits her grip,
And carping Envy silent bites her lip.

Lines

WRITTEN ON SEEING A SPIDER DART OUT UPON A FLY.

LET gang your grip, ye auld grim devil !
Else with ae crush I'll mak' you civil :
Like debtor-bard in merchant's claw,
The fient o' mercy ye've at a' !
Sae spite an' malice (hard to ken 'em,)
Sit spewing out their secret venom ;—
Ah, hear !—poor buzzard's roaring murder ;
Let gang !—Na faith !—Thou scorn'st my order !—
Weel, tak' thou that !—vile ruthless creature !
For who but hates a savage nature ?
Sic fate to ilk unsocial kebar,
Who lays a snare to wrang his neighbour.

Lines

ON SEEING A FOP PASS AN OLD BEGGAR.

HE who, unmov'd, can hear the suppliant cry
  Of pallid wretch, plac'd on the pathway side,
Nor deigns one pitying look, but passes by
  In all the pomp of self-adorning pride—
So may some great man vex his little soul,
  When he, obsequies, makes his lowest bow :
Turn from him with a look that says, " Vain fool,"
  And speak to some poor man whom he would shame **to**
    know.

Parody on "Lullaby."

WRITTEN ON SEEING THE LATE MR THOMAS WILLOUGHBY, TRAGEDIAN,
RATHER BELOW HIMSELF.

PEACEFUL, slumb'ring in the ale-house,
   See the god-like Rolla lie;
Drink outwits the best of fellows:
   Here lies poor Tom Willoughby.

Where is stern King Richard's fury?
   Where is Osmond's blood-flush'd eye?
See these mighty men before ye,
   Sunk to poor Tom Willoughby.

Pity 'tis that men of merit,
   Thus such sterling worth destroy;
O ye gods! did I inherit
   Half the pow'rs of Willoughby.

Lines

ON A FLATTERER.

I HATE a flatterer as I hate the devil,
   But Tom's a very, very pleasant dog;
Of course let's speak of him in terms more civil—
   I hate a flatterer as I hate a hog:
Not but applause is music to mine ears,
   He is a knave who says he likes it not,
But when in Friendship's guise Deceit appears,
   'Twould fret a Stoic's frigid temper hot.

A Resolve.

WRITTEN ON HEARING A FELLOW TELL SOME STORIES TO THE HURT OF
HIS BEST FRIENDS.

As secret's the grave be the man whom I trust;
   What friendship imparts still let honour conceal:
A plague on those babblers, their names be accurs'd!
   Still first to inquire, and the first to reveal.

As open as day let me be with the man
· Who tells me my failings from motives upright ;
But when of those gossipping fools I meet one,
    Let me fold in my soul, and be close as the night.

Lines

WRITTEN WITH A PENCIL IN A TAP-ROOM.

This warld's a tap-room owre and owre,
    Whare ilk ane tak's his caper ;
Some taste the sweet, some drink the sour,
    As waiter Fate sees proper.
Let mankind live ae social core,
    And drap a' selfish quarr'lling,
And when the landlord ca's his score,
    May ilk ane's clink be sterling.

Epistle to James Scadlock.

WRITTEN ON RECEIVING FROM HIM A SMALL MS. VOLUME OF ORIGINAL
SCOTTISH POEMS.

April, 1803

When colleged bards bestride Pegasus,
And try to gallop up Parnassus,
    By dint o' mickle lear,
The lowe o' friendship fires my soul,
To write you this poetic scrawl,
    Prosaic, dull, I fear !
        But weel I ken your generous heart
        Will overlook its failings,
        And where the poet has come short
        Let friendship cure his ailings,
            'Tis kind, man—divine, man,
            To hide the fault we see,
            Or try to men't, as far's we ken't,
            Wi' true sincerity.

This last observe brings i' my head
To tell you here my social creed :
    Let's use a' mankind weel ;
And ony sumph who'd use us ill,
Wi' dry contempt let's treat him still ;

He'll feel it worst himsel' :
I never flatter, praise but rare ;
  I scorn a double part;
And when I speak I speak sincere,
  The dictates o' my heart.
    I truly hate the dirty gate
      That mony a body tak's.
    Wha fraze ane, syne blaze ane,
      As soon's they turn their backs.
In judging, let us be right hooly :

I've heard some folks descant sae freely
  On other people's matters,
As if themselves were real perfection,
When, had they stood a fair inspection,
  The abused were far their betters.
    But gossips aye maun hae their crack,
      Though moralists should rail ;
    Let's end the matter wi' this fact,
      That goodness pays itsel'.
      The joys, man, that raise man
        To ane frae doing weel,
      Are siccan joys that hardened vice
        Can seldom ever feel.

Oh, Jamie, man ! I'm proud to see't,
Our ain auld muse yet keeps her feet,
  'Maist healthy as before ;
For sad predicting fears foretauld,
When Robin's glowing heart turned cauld,
  Then a' our joys were o'er.
    Ilk future bard revere his name,
      Through thousand years to come ;
    And though we cannot reach his fame,
      Busk laurels round his tomb.
      Yet, though he's dead, the Scottish reed
        This mony a day may ring,
      In Livingston, in Anderson,
        In Scadlock, and in King.

"The Tap-room," what a glorious treat!
"Complaint and Wish," how plaintive sweet !
  "The Weaver's" just "Lament ;"

The gloamin' fragment, how divine!
There nature speaks in every line;
  The bard's immortal in't.
     Yon " Epigram on Jamie Long"
      Is pointed as the steel;
     And " Hoot! ye ken yoursel' " 's a song
      Would please e'en Burns himsel'!
       Let snarling mean quarrelling,
        Be doubly damned henceforth!
       An l let us raise the voice of praise,
        To hearten modest worth.

And you, my dear respected frien',
Your " Spring" 's a precious evergreen,
  Fresh beauties budding still:
Your " Levern Banks" and " Killoch Burn,"
Ye sing them wi' sae sweet a turn,
  Ye gar the heart-strings thrill.
     "October winds," e'en let them rave
      Wi' nature-blasting howl,
    If in return kind heaven give
    The sunshine of the soul:
       The feeling heart that bears a part
       In others' joys and woes,
       May still depend to find a friend,
       Howe'er the tempest blows.

Yet, long I've thought, and think it yet,
True friends are rarely to be met
  Who share in others' troubles;
Who jointly joy, or drop the tear
Reciprocal, and kindly bear
  Wi' ane another's troubles.
     Even such a friend I once could boast,
      Ah! now in death he's low;
    But fond anticipation hopes
    For such a friend in you.
       Dear Jamie, forgie me
        That last presumptive line;
       See, here's my hand at your command
        Ye hae my heart langsyne!

The Moralists.

"BARBAROUS!" cried John, in humanizing mood,
To Will, who'd shot a blackbird in the wood;
"The savage Indian pleads necessity,
But thou, barbarian wretch! hast no such plea."
Hark! click the alehouse door, his wife comes in:
"Dear help's, man, John! preserve me, what d'ye mean?
Six helpless bairns, the deil confound your drouth,
Without ae bit to stap a single mouth."
"Get hame," cried John, "else, jade, I'll kick your a—e,"
Sure such humanity is all a farce.

Lines

WRITTEN ON THE BACK OF A GUINEA NOTE.

THOU little badge of independence,
Thou mak'st e'en pride dance mean attendance;
Thou sure hast magic in thy looks,
Gives poets a taste for tasteless books;
Mak'st lawyers lie, mak'st courtiers flatter,
And wily statesmen patriots clatter.
Mak'st ancient maids seem young again,
At sixty beauteous as sixteen;
Mak'st foes turn friends, and friends turn foes,
And drugmen brew the poisoning dose;
And even, as common say prevails,
Thou mak'st e'en justice tip the scales.

Lines

ON A COUNTRY JUSTICE IN THE SOUTH.

WHAT gars yon gentry gang wi' Jock,
And ca' him sir and master?
The greatest dunce, the biggest block,
That ever nature cuist her:
Yet see, they've placed this human stock
Strict justice to dispense;
Which plainly shows, yon meikle folk
Think siller stands for sense.

A Lesson.

QUOTH gobbin Tom of Lancashire,
   To northern Jock, a lowland drover,
"Those are foin kaise thai'rt driving there,
   They've zure been fed on English clover."
"Foin kaise!" quoth Jock, "ye bleth'ring hash,
   Deil draw your nose as lang's a sow's!
That tauk o' yours is queer-like trash,
   Foin kaise! poor gowk!—their names are KOOSE."
The very fault which I in others see,
Like kind, or worse, perhaps, is seen in me.

Epigrams.

CRIED Dick to Bob, "Great news to-day!"
"Great news," quoth Bob, "what great news, pray?"
Said Dick, "Our gallant tars at sea,
Have gain'd a brilliant victory."
"Indeed!" cried Bob, "it may be true,
But that, you know, is nothing new."

"FRENCH threats of invasion let Britons defy,
   And spike the proud frogs if our coast they should
     crawl on."
Yes, statesmen know well that our spirits are high,
   The financier has rais'd them two shillings per gallon.

NATURE, impartial in her ends,
   When she made man the strongest,
For scrimpet pith, to mak' amends,
   Made woman's tongue the longest.

Epitaphs.

ON SEEING A ONCE WORTHY CHARACTER LYING INEBRIATED ON THE STREET.

IF loss of worth may draw the pity tear,
Stop, passenger, and pay that tribute here—
Here lies whom all with justice did commend,
The rich man's pattern, and the poor man's friend ;
He cheer'd pale Indigence's bleak abode,
He oft removed Misfortune's galling load ;
Nor was his bounty to one sect confined,
His goodness beam'd alike on all mankind :
Now, lost in folly, all his virtues sleep—
Let's mind his former worth, and o'er his frailties weep.

FOR T—— B——, ESQ.

A GENTLEMAN WHOM INDIGENCE NEVER SOLICITED IN VAIN.

EVER green be the sod o'er kind Tom of the Wood,
    For the poor man he ever supplied ;
We may weel say, alas ! for our ain scant of grace,
    That we reck'd not his worth till he died ;
Though no rich marble bust mimics grief o'er his dust,
    Yet fond memory his virtues will save ;
Oft, at lone twilight hour, sad remembrance shall pour
    Her sorrows, unfeigned, o'er his grave.

ON A CRABBED OLD MAID.

HERE slaethorn Mary's hurcheon bouk,
    Resigns its fretful bristles :
And is she dead ? No—reader, look,
    Her grave's o'ergrown wi' thistles.

ON A FARTHING GATHERER.

HERE lies Jamie Wight, wha was wealthy and proud,
Few shar'd his regard, and far fewer his goud ;
He lived unesteem'd, and he died unlamented,
The kirk gat his gear, and auld Jamie is sainted.

Epistle to James King,

ON RECEIVING A MORAL EPISTLE FROM HIM.—MAY, 1802.

PLEASE accept the thanks and praise
Due to your poetic lays;
Wisdom aye should be rever'd,
Sense to wit be aye preferr'd.
   Just your thoughts in simple guise,
Fit to make frail mortals wise;
Every period, every line,
With some moral truth doth shine.
   Like the rocks, which storms divide,
Thund'ring down the mountain side,
So strides Time, with rapid force,
Round his unobstructed course;
Like a flood upon its way,
Sweeping downward to the sea:
But what figure so sublime,
As describe the flight of time?
   Life's a dream, and man's a bubble
Compass'd round with care and trouble:
Like a ship in tempest tost,
Soon o'erwhelm'd, for ever lost;
Like the short-liv'd passion-flow'r,
Blooming, dying in an hour;
Like the tuneful bird that sings,
Flutt'ring high on sportive wings;
Till the fowler's subtle art,
Drives Death's message to its heart,
While, perhaps, Death aims his blow,
Swift to lay the wretch as low.
   Now, since life is but a day,
Make the most of it we may;
Calm and tranquil let us be,
Still resigned to Fate's decree.
Let not poortith sink us low,
Let not wealth exalt our brow;
Let's be grateful, virtuous, wise:
There's where all our greatness lies.

Doing all the good we can,
Is all that Heaven requires of man.
   Wherefore should we grieve and sigh,
'Cause we know that we must die?
Death's a debt requir'd by nature,
To be paid by every creature.
Rich and poor, and high and low,
Fall by Death's impartial blow.
God, perhaps, in kindness will
Snatch us from some coming ill;
Death may kindly waft us o'er
To a milder, happier shore.
   But, dear Jamie, after a',
What I've said's not worth a straw
What is't worth to moralize
What we never can practise?
As for me, with a' my skill,
Passion leads me as she will;
And resolves, laid down to-day,
Ere to-morrow, 're done away:
   Then, let's ever cheerie live,
Do our best, and never grieve;
Still let Friendship's warmest tie
All deficiencies supply.
And, while favour'd by the Nine,
I your laurels will entwine.

Epistle to James Barr,

WHEREVER HE MAY BE FOUND.—MARCH, 1804.

GUDE Pibrocharian, jorum-jirger,
Say, ha'e ye turn'd an Antiburgher?
Or lang-fac'd Presbyterian elder,
Deep read in wiles o' gathering siller?
Or cauld splenetic solitair,
Resolved to herd wi' man nae mair?
   As to the second, I've nae fear for't,
For siller, faith ye ne'er did care for't,
Unless to help a needfu' body,

And get an antrin glass o' toddy.
But what the black mischief's come owre you?
These three months I've been speirin' for you,
Till e'en the Muse, wi' downright grieving,
Has worn her chafts as thin's a shaving.
Say, ha'e ye ta'en a tramp to Lon'on,
In Co. wi' worthy auld Buchanan?
Wha mony a mile wad streek his shanks
To ha'e a crack wi' Josie Banks,
Concerning shells, and birds, and metals,
Moths, spiders, butterflies, and beetles.
For you, I think, ye'll cut a figure,
Wi' king o' pipers, Malc. M'Gregor.
And wi' your clarion, flute, and fiddle,
Will gar their southron heart-strings diddle.

   Or are you through the kintra whisking,
Accoutred wi' the sock and buskin?
Thinking to climb to wealth and fame,
By adding Roscius to your name?
Frae thoughts o' that, pray, keep abeigh!
Ye're far owre auld, and far owre heigh;
Since in thir novel-hunting days,
There's nane but bairns can act our plays.
At twal-year auld, if ye had tried it,
I doubtna but ye might succeeded;
But full-grown buirdly chields like you,
Quite monstrous, man, 'twill never do!

   Or are ye gane, as there are few sic,
For teaching of a band o' music?
Oh, hear auld Scotland's fervent prayers!
And teach her genuine native airs;
Whilk simply play'd, devoid o' art,
Thrill through the senses to the heart.
Play, when you'd rouse the patriot's saul,
True valour's tune, "The Garb of Gaul."
And when laid low in glory's bed,
Let " Roslin Castle" soothe his shade.
The " Bonnie bush aboon Traquair,"
Its every accent breathes despair;
And " Ettrick Banks," celestial strain!
Mak's simmer's gloaming mair serene;
And, oh, how sweet the plaintive muse,

Amang "The Broom o' Cowdenknowes!"
To hear the love-lorn swain complain,
Lone on "The Braes o' Ballendine;"
It e'en might melt the dortiest she,
That ever sklented scornfu' e'e.
When Beauty tries her vocal pow'rs
Amang the green-wood's echoing bow'rs,
The "Bonnie Birks of Invermay"
Might mend a seraph's sweetest lay.
Then, should grim Care invest your castle,
Just knock him down wi' "Willie Wastle,"
And rant blythe "Lumps o' puddin'" owre him,
And for his dirge sing "Tullochgorum."
When Orpheus charm'd his wife frae hell,
'Twas nae Scotch tune he play'd sae well;
Else had the worthy auld wire-scraper
Been keepet for his de'ilship's piper.
　Or if ye've turned a feather'd fop,
Light dancing upon fashion's top,
Wi' lofty brow and selfish e'e,
Despising low-clad dogs like me;
Uncaring your contempt or favour,
Sweet butterfly, adieu for ever!
But, hold,—I'm wrong to doubt your sense,
For pride proceeds from ignorance.
If peace of mind lay in fine clothes,
I'd be the first of fluttering beaux,
And strut as proud as ony peacock
That ever crawed on top o' hay-cock;
And ere I'd know one vexing thought,
Get dollar buttons on my coat,
Wi' a the lave o' fulsome trash on,
That constitutes a man of fashion.
Oh, grant me this, kind Providence:
A moderate, decent competence;
Thou'lt see me smile, in independence,
Above weak-sauled, pride-born ascendence,
　But whether ye're gane to teach the whistle,
'Midst noise and rough reg'mental bustle;
Or gane to strut upon the stage,
Smit wi' the mania o' the age;
Or Scotchman-like ha'e tramp'd abreed,

To yon big town, far south the Tweed;
Or dourin' in the hermit's cell,
Unblessing and unblessed yoursel';
In Gude's name write!—tak' up your pen,
A' how ye're doing let me ken,
Sae hoping, quickly, your epistle,
Adieu! thou genuine son of song and whistle.

POSTCRIPT.

We had a concert here short syne,
Oh, man! the music was divine,
Baith plaintive sang and merry glee,
In a' the soul of harmony.
When Smith and Stewart leave this earth,
The gods, in token o' their worth,
Will welcome them at heaven's portals,
The brightest, truest, best o' mortals.
Apollo proud, as weel he may,
Will walk on tip-toe a' that day;
While a' the muses kindred claim,
Rememb'ring what they've done for them.

Epistle to James Scadloch,

THEN AT PERTH—JUNE, 1804.

LET those who never felt its flame,
Say friendship is an empty name;
    Such selfish, cauld philosophy,
    For ever I disclaim.

It soothes the soul with grief oppressed,
Half-cures the care-distemper'd breast,
    And in the jocund happy hour,
    Gives joy a higher zest.

All nature sadden'd at our parting hour,
Winds plaintive howl'd, clouds weeping, dropt a show'r;
    Our fields look'd dead, as if they'd said,
    We ne'er shall see him more!

Though fate and fortune threw their darts,
Envying us your high deserts,
    They well might tear you from our arms,
    But never from our hearts.

When spring buds forth in vernal show'rs,
When summer comes arrayed in flow'rs,
    Or autumn kind, from Ceres' horn,
    Her grateful bounty pours.

Or bearded winter curls his brow,
I'll often fondly think on you,
    And on our happy days and nights,
    With pleasing back-cast view.

If e'er in musing mood ye stray,
Alang the banks of classic Tay,
    Think on our walks by Stanley tow'r,
    And steep Gleniffer brae.

Think on our langsyne happy hours,
Spent where the burn wild rapid pours,
    And o'er the horrid dizzy steep,
    Dashes her mountain-stores.

Think on our walks by sweet Greenlaw,
By woody hill and birken shaw,
    Where nature strews her choicest sweets
    To mak' the landscape braw.

And think on rural Ferguslie,
Its plantings green and flow'ry lea ;
    Such fairy scenes, though distant far,
    May please the mental e'e.

Yon mentor, Geordie Zimmerman,
Agrees exactly with our plan ;
    That partial hours of solitude
    Exalt the soul of man.

So, oft retir'd from strife and din,
Let's shun the jarring ways of men,
    And seek serenity and peace
    By stream and woody glen.

But e'er a few short summers gae,
Your friend will meet his kindred clay ;
    For fell disease tugs at my breast,
    To hurry me away.

Yet while life's bellows bear to blaw,
Till life's last lang-fetched breath I draw,
    I'll often fondly think on you,
    And mind your kindness a'.

Now fare-ye-weel ! still may ye find
A friend congenial to your mind,
    To share your joys and half your woes,
    Warm, sympathizing, kind.

Epistle to William Thomson,

AT OVERTON,—JUNE, 1805.

DEAR WILL, my much respect'd frien',
I send you this to let you ken
That, though at distance fate hath set you,
Your friends in Paisley don't forget you ;
But often think on you, far lone,
Amang the braes of Overton.
    Our social club continues yet,
Perpetual source of mirth and wit ;
Our rigid rules admit but few,
Yet still we'll keep a chair for you.
    A country life I've oft envied,
Where love, and truth, and peace preside :
Without temptations to allure,
Your days glide on unstained and pure ;
Nae midnight revels waste your health,
Nor greedy landlord drains your wealth ;
Ye're never fashed wi' whisky fever,
Nor dizzy pow, nor dullness ever ;
But breathe the halesome caller air,
Remote from aught that genders care.
    I needna' tell how much I lang
To hear your rural Scottish sang ;
To hear you sing your heath-clad braes,

Your jocund nights and happy days ;
And lilt wi' glee the blythesome morn,
When dewdraps pearl every thorn ;
When larks pour forth the early sang,
And lintwhites chant the whins amang.
And pyats hap frae tree to tree,
Teaching their young anes how to flee ;
While frae the mavis to the wren,
A' warble sweet in bush or glen.
   In town we scarce can find occasion
To note the beauties o' creation ;
But study mankind's different dealings,
Their virtues, vices, merits, failings.
Unpleasing task compared wi' yours :
You range the hills 'mang mountain flow'rs,
And view afar the smoky town,
More bless'd than all its riches were your own.
   A lang epistle I might scribble,
But aiblins ye will grudge the trouble
Of reading sic low hamewart rhyme,
And sae it's best to quat in time ;
Sae I, with soul sincere and fervent,
Am still you trustful friend and servant.

Epistle to William Wylie.

JANUARY, 1806.

DEAR kindred saul, thanks to the cause
   First made us ken each other ;
Ca't fate, or chance, I care not whilk,
   To me it brought a brother.

Thy furthy, kindly, takin' gait :
   Sure every guid chield likes thee,
And bad luck wring his thrawart heart,
   Wha snarling e'er would vex thee.

Though mole-ey'd Fortune's partial hand,
   O' clink may keep thee bare o't ;
Of what thou hast, pale Misery
   Receives, unasked, a share o't.

Thou gi'est without ae hank'ring thought,
　　Or cauld, self-stinted wish ;
E'en winter-finger'd Avarice
　　Approves thee with a blush.

If grief e'er mak' thee her packhorse,
　　Her leaden load to carry't,
Shove half the burden on my back,
　　I'll do my best to bear it.

Guid kens we a' ha'e faults enew,
　　'Tis Friendship's task to cure 'em ;
But still she spurns the critic view,
　　And bids us to look o'er 'em.

When Death performs his beadle part,
　　And summons thee to heaven,
By virtue of thy warm, kind heart,
　　Thy faults will be forgiven.

And shouldst thou live to see thy friend
　　Borne lifeless on the bier ;
I ask of thee for epitaph,
　　One kind elegaic tear.

Epistle to Alexander Borland.

GLASGOW.—FEBRUARY, 1806.

RETIR'D disgusted from the tavern roar,
Where strong-lung'd Ignorance does highest soar;
Where silly ridicule is pass'd for wit,
And shallow Laughter takes her gaping fit;
Here lone I sit, in musing melancholy,
Resolv'd for aye to shun the court of Folly ;
For, from whole years' experience in her train,
One hour of joy brings twenty hours of pain.
Now since I'm on the would-be better key,
The Muse oft whispers me to write to thee,
Not that she means a self-debasing letter,
But merely show there's hope I may turn better;
That what stands bad to my account of ill,
You may set down to passion, not to will.

The fate-scourg'd exile, destined still to roam
Through desert wilds, far from his early home,—
If some fair prospect meet his sorrowing eyes,
Like that he own'd beneath his native skies,
Sad recollection, murdering relief,
He bursts in all the agonies of grief ;
Mem'ry presents the volume of his care,
And harrows up his soul with " such things were."
'Tis so in life—when Youth folds up his page,
And turns the leaf to dark, blank, joyless age,
Where sad Experience speaks in language plain,
Her thoughts of bliss, and highest hopes were vain:
O'er present ills I think I see her mourn,
And " weep past joys that never will return."
   Then come, my friend, while yet in life's gay noon,
Ere grief's dark clouds obscure our summer sun,
Ere winter's sleety blasts around us howl,
And chill our every energy of soul :
Let us look back, retrace the ways we've trod,
Mark virtue's paths from guilty pleasure's road,
And, 'stead of wand'ring in a devious maze,
Mark some few precepts for our future days.
   I mind still well, when but a trifling boy,
My young heart flutter'd with a savage joy,
As with my sire I wander'd through the wood,
And found the mavis' clump-lodged callow brood:
I tore them thence, exulting o'er my prize,
My father bade me list the mother's cries.
" So thine would wail," he said, " if reft of thee :"
It was a lesson of humanity.
   Not to recount our every early joy,
When all was happiness without alloy ;
Nor tread again each flow'ry field we traced,
Light as the silk-winged butterflies we chased ;
Ere villain falsehood taught the glowing mind,
To look with cold suspicion on mankind—
Let's pass the valley of our younger years,
And farther up-hill mark what now appears.
   We see the sensualist, fell vice's slave,
Fatigu'd, worn out, sink to an early grave;
We see the slave of av'rice grind the poor,
His thirst for gold increasing with his store ;

Pack-horse of fortune, all his days are care,
Her burdens bearing to his spendthrift heir.
   Next view the spendthrift, joyous o'er his purse,
Exchanging all his guineas for remorse ;
On pleasure's flow'r-deck'd barge away he's borne,
Supine, till every flow'r starts up a thorn.
Then all his pleasures fly, like air-borne bubbles :
He ruined sinks amidst a sea of troubles.
   Hail, Temperance, thou'rt wisdom's first, best lore,
The sage in every age does thee adore ;
Within thy pale we taste of ev'ry joy,
O'erstepping that, our highest pleasures cloy :
The heart-enlivening, friendly, social bowl,
To rap'trous ecstasy exalts the soul ;
But when to midnight hour we keep it up,
Next morning feels the poison of the cup.
   Though fate forbade the gifts of schoolmen mine,
With classic art to write the polish'd line,
Yet miners oft must gather earth with gold,
And truth may strike, though e'er so roughly told.
   If thou in aught would'st rise to eminence,
Show not the faintest shadow of pretence,
Else busy Scandal, with her hundred tongues,
Will quickly find thee in ten thousand wrongs ;
Each strives to tear his neighbour's honour down,
As if detracting something from his own.
Of all the ills with which mankind are curs'd,
An envious, discontented mind's the worst ;
There muddy Spleen exalts her gloomy throne,
Marks all conditions better than her own :
Hence Defamation spreads her ant-bear tongue,
And grimly pleas'd, feeds on another's wrong.
Curse on the wretch who, when his neighbour's bless'd,
Erects his peace-destroying, snaky crest !
And him who sits in surly, sullen mood,
Repining at a fellow-mortal's good !
Man owns so little of true happiness,
That cursed be he who makes that little less.
   The zealot thinks he'll go to heaven direct,
Adhering to the tenets of his sect,
E'en though his practice lie in this alone,

To rail at all persuasions but his own.
In judging, still let moderation guide;
O'erheated zeal is certain to mislead.
First bow to God in heart-warm gratitude,
Next do our utmost for the general good.
In spite of all the forms which men devise,
'Tis there where real solid wisdom lies;
And impious is the man who claims dominion,
To damn his neighbour diff'ring in opinion.
When suppliant Misery greets thy wand'ring eye,
Although in public, pass not heedless by;
Distress impels her to implore the crowd,
For that denied within her lone abode.
Give thou the trifling pittance which she craves,
Though ostentation called by prudent knaves;
So conscience will a rich reward impart,
And finer feelings play around the heart.
When Wealth with arrogance exalts his brow,
And reckons Poverty a wretch most low,
Let good intentions dignify thy soul,
And conscious rectitude will crown the whole.
Hence indigence will independence own,
And soar above the haughty despot's frown.
Still to thy lot be virtuously resigned;
Above all treasures prize thy peace of mind;
Then let not envy rob thy soul of rest,
Nor discontent e'er harbour in thy breast.
Be not too fond of popular applause,
Which often echoes in a villain's cause,
Whose specious sophistry gilds his deceit,
Till power abused, in time shows forth the cheat:
Yet be't thy pride to bear an honest fame;
More dear than life watch over thy good name;
For he, poor man! who has no wish to gain it,
Despises all the virtues which attain it.
Of friendship, still be secrecy the test,
This maxim let be 'graven in my breast:
Whate'er a friend enjoins me to conceal,
I'm weak, I'm base, if I the same reveal.
Let honour, acting as a powerful spell,
Suppress that itching fondness still to tell;
Else, unthank'd chronicle, the cunning's tool,

The world will stamp me for a gossip fool.
Yet let us act an honest open part,
Nor curb the warm effusions of the heart,
Which, naturally virtuous, discommends
Aught mean or base, even in our dearest friends.
　　But why this long disjointed scrawl to thee,
Whose every action is a law to me ;
Whose every deed proclaims thy noble mind,
Industrious. independent, just, and kind ?
Methinks I hear thee say, " Each fool may teach,
Since now my whim-led friend's begun to preach."
But this first essay of my preaching strain,
Hear and accept, for friendship's sake.   Amen.

─────────

Epistle to James Buchanan.

KILBARCHAN.—AUGUST, 1806.

My guid auld friend on Locher banks,
Your kindness claims my warmest thanks;
Yet, thanks is but a draff-cheap phrase,
Of little value now-a-days :
Indeed, 'tis hardly worth the heeding,
Unless to show a body's breeding.
Yet many a poor doiled servile body,
Will scrimp his stomach of its crowdy,
And pride to run a great man's errands,
And feed on smiles and sour cheese parings,
And think himsel' na sma sheep-shank,
Rich laden wi' his lordship's thank.
The sodger, too, for a' his troubles,
His hungry wames, and bluidy hubbles,
His agues, rheumatisms, cramps,
Receiv'd in plashy winter camps,
Oh. blest reward! at last he gains
His sovereign's thanks for a' his pains.
　　Thus, though 'mang first o' friends I rank you,
'Twere but sma' compliment to thank you ;
Yet, lest ye think me here ungratefu',
Of hatefu' names, a name most hatefu',

The neist time that you come to toun,
By a' the powers beneath the moon,
I'll treat you wi' a Highland gill,
Though it should be my hindmost fill!
　　Though in the bustling town, the Muse
Has gather'd little feck o' news:
'Tis said, the Court of Antiquarians
Has split on some great point o' variance;
For ane has got in gouden box,
The spectacles of auld John Knox;
A second proudly thanks his fate wi'
The hindmaist pen that Nelson wrote wi';
A third ane owns an antique rare,
A sape-brush made o' mermaid's hair!
But, niggard wights! they a' refuse 'em,
These precious relics, to the museum,
Whilk selfish, mean, illegal deeds,
Ha'e set them a' at loggerheads.
　　Sure taste refin'd and public spirit,
Stand next to genius and merit:
I'm proud to see your warm regard,
For Caledonia's dearest bard:
Of him ye've got sae guid a painting,
That nought but real life is wanting.
I think yon rising genius, Tannock,*
May gain a niche in Fame's high winnock;
There, with auld Reubens, placed sublime,
Look down upon the wreck of time.
　　I ne'er, as yet, ha'e found a patron,
For, scorn be til't, I hate a' flatt'rin';
Besides, I never had an itchin'
To slake about a great man's kitchen,
And like a spaniel lick his dishes,
And come and gang just to his wishes:
Yet studious to give worth its due,
I pride to praise the like of you;
Guid chiels, replete wi' sterling sense,
Wha' wi' their worth mak' nae pretence.
Aye, there's my worthy friend M'Math,
I'll lo'e him till my latest breath,
And like a traitor-wretch be hanged,

* The painter of Burns' portrait is here referred to.

Before I'd hear that fellow wranged :
His every action shows his mind,
Humanely noble, bright, and kind :
And here's the worth o't, doubly rooted,
He never speaks ae word about it.
My compliments and warm guid-will,
To Maisters Simpson, Barr, and Lyle.
Wad rav'ning Time but spare my pages,
They'd tell the warl in after ages,
That it to me was wealth and fame,
To be esteemed by chiels like them.
O Time, thou all-devouring bear !
Hear—" List, oh list " my ardent pray'r !
I crave thee here, on bended knee,
To let my dear-loved pages be ;
Oh ! take thy sharp-nailed, nibbling elves,
To musty scrolls on college shelves ;
There, with dry treatises on law,
Feast, cram, and gorge thy greedy maw ;
But grant, amidst thy thin-sown mercies,
To spare, oh spare my darling verses !
　　Could I but up through hist'ry wimple,
Wi' Robertson, or sage Dalrymple ;
Or had I half the pith and lear
Of a Mackenzie, or a Blair ;
I aiblins then might tell some story
Wad show the Muse in bleezing glory ;
But scrimp'd o' time, and lear scholastic,
My lines limp on in Hudibrastic,
Till Hope, grown sick, flings down her claim,
And drops her dreams o' future fame.
Yes, oh waesucks ! should I be vauntie ?
My Muse is just a Rosinante :
She stammers forth, wi' hilching canter,
Sagely intent on strange adventure ;
Yet, sae uncouth in garb and feature,
　She seems the fool of Literature.
But lest the critic's birsie besom,
Swoop off this cant of egotism,
I'll sidelins hint—na, bauldly tell,
I whiles think something o' mysel':
Else, wha the de'il wad fash to scribble,

Expecting scorn for a' his trouble ?
Yet, lest dear self should be mista'en,
I'll fling the bridle o'er the mane ;
For after a', I fear this jargon
Is but a Willie Glassford bargain.

Epistle to Robert Allan.

KILBARCHAN.—1807.

DEAR ROBIN,
  THE Muse is now a wee at leisure,
An' sits her down wi' meikle pleasure,
To skelp you aff a blaud o' rhyme,
As near's she can to true sublime ;
But here's the rub,—poor poet-devils,
We're compassed round wi' mony evils ;
We jerk oursel's into a fever
To give the world something clever,
An' after a' perhaps we muddle
In vile prosaic stagnant puddle.
For me—I seldom choose a subject,
My rhymes are oft without an object ;
I let the Muse e'en tak' her win',
And dash awa' thro' thick and thin:
For Method's sic a servile creature,
She spurns the wilds o' simple nature
An' paces on, wi' easy art,
A lang day's journey frae the heart:—
Sae what comes uppermaist you'll get it,
Be't good or ill, for you I write it.
  How fares my worthy friend, the bard ?
Be peace and honour his reward !
May ev'ry ill that gars us fyke,
Bad webs, toom pouches, and sic like,
An' ought that would his spirit bend,
Be ten miles distant from my friend.
Alas ! this wicked endless war,
Rul'd by some vile malignant star,
Has sunk poor Britain low indeed,
Has robb'd Industry o' her bread,

An' dash'd the sair-won cog o' crowdie
Frae mony an honest eident body;
While Genius, dying through neglect,
Sinks down amidst the general wreck
Just like twa cats tied tail to tail,
They worry at it tooth and nail;
They girn, they bite in deadly wrath,
An' what is't for? for nought in faith!
Wee Lourie Frank* wi' brazen snout,
Nae doubt would like to scart us out,
For proud John Bull, aye us'd to hone him,
We'll no gi'e o'er to spit upon him,
But Lourie's rais'd to sic degree,
John would be wise to let him be;
Else aiblins, as he's wearin' aul',
Frank yet may tear him spawl frae spawl,
For wi' the mony chirts he's gotten,
I fear his *constitution's* rotten.
But while the bullying blades o' Europe
Are boxing ither to a syrup,
Let's mind oursel's as weel's we can,
An' live in peace, like man and man,
An' no cast out and fecht like brutes,
Without a cause for our disputes.
When I read o'er your kind epistle,
I didna dance, nor sing, nor whistle,
But jump'd, and cried, Huzza! huzza!
Like Robin Roughead in the play;—
But to be serious—jest aside,
I felt a glow o' secret pride,
Thus to be roos'd by ane like you;
Yet doubted if sic praise was due,
Till self thus reason'd in the matter:
Ye ken that Robin scorns to flatter,
And ere he'd prostitute his quill,
He'd rather burn his rhyming mill—
Enough! I cried—I've gain'd my end,
Since I ha'e pleased my worthy friend.
My sangs are now before the warl',
An' some may praise, and some may snarl;
They ha'e their faults, yet I can tell

* A personification of France.

Nane sees them clearer than mysel';
But still, I think, they too inherit
Amang the dross some sparks o' merit.
 Then come, my dear Parnassian brither,
Let's lay our poet heads thegither,
And sing our ain sweet native scenes,
Our streams, our banks, and rural plains,
Our woods, our shaws, and flow'ry holms,
An' mountains clad wi' purple blooms,
Wi' burnies bickerin' down their braes,
Reflecting back the sunny rays;
Ye've Semple Woods, and Calder Glen,
And Locher Bank, sweet fairy den!
And Auchenames a glorious theme!
Where Crawford* liv'd, of deathless name,
Where Sempill† sued his lass to win,
And Nelly rose and let him in
Where Habbie Simpson‡ lang did play,
The first o' pipers in his day;
And though aneath the turf langsyne,
Their sangs and tunes shall never tyne.
 Sae, Robin, briskly ply the Muse;
She warms our hearts, expands our views,
Gars every sordid passion flee,
And waukens every sympathy.
 Now, wishing Fate may never tax you,
Wi' cross, nor loss, to thraw and vex you,
But keep you hale till ninety-nine,
Till you and yours in honour shine;
Shall ever be my earnest prayer,
While I've a friendly wish to spare.

* Wm. Crawford, a Scottish poet, author of "Tweedside," "The bush aboon Traquair," &c., died about 1730.
 † Francis Semple, a Scottish poet, author of "Maggie Lauder," "The blythsome bridal," &c.
 ‡ A celebrated piper of Kilbarchan.

Towser;

A TRUE TALE.

" Dogs are honest creatures,
  Ne'er fawn on any that they love not;
  And I'm a friend to dogs;
  They ne'er betray their masters."

In mony an instance, without doubt,
The man may copy from the brute,
And by th' example grow much wiser;
Then read the short memoirs of Towser.
  With deference to our great Lavaters,
Wha judge o' mankind by their features,
There's mony a smiling, pleasant-faced cock,
That wears a heart no worth a castock;
While mony a visage, antic, droll,
O'erveils a noble, generous soul.
With Towser this was just the case,
He had an ill-faur'd, tawted face;
His make was something like a messan,
But big, and quite unprepossessin';
His master coft him frae some fallows,
Who had him doomed unto the gallows,
Because (sae hap'd poor Towser's lot)
He wudna tear a comrade's throat;
Yet in affairs of love or honour,
He'd stand his part amang a hun'er;
And where'er fighting was a merit,
He never failed to show his spirit.
He never girn'd in neighbour's face,
With wild ill-natur'd scant of grace;
Nor e'er accosted ane with smiles,
Then, soon as turn'd, wad bite his heels:
Nor ever kent the courtier art,
To fawn with rancour at his heart;
Nor aught kent he of cankert quar'lling,
Nor snarling just for sake o' snarling;
Ye'd pinch him sair afore he'd growl,
Whilk shows he had a mighty soul.
  But what adds maistly to his fame,
And will immortalize his name—

" Immortalize !—presumptuous wight !
Thy lines are dull as darkest night,
Without ae spark o' wit or glee,
To light them through futurity."
E'en be it sae ;—poor Towser's story,
Though lamely tauld, will speak his glory.
   'Twas in the month o' cauld December,
When nature's fire seemed just an ember,
And growling winter bellow'd forth,
In storms and tempests frae the north ;
When honest Towser's loving master,
Regardless o' the surly bluster,
Set out to the neist borough town,
To buy some needments of his own ;
And, case some purse-pest should way-lay him,
He took his trusty servant wi' him.
   His business done 'twas near the gloaming,
And aye the king o' storms was foaming ;
The doors did ring—lum-pigs down tumbled,
The strands gushed big—the sinks loud rumbled ;
Auld grannies spread their looves and sighed,
Wi' " Oh, sirs ! what an awfu' night !"
Poor Towser shook his side a' draigl'd,
An's master grudged that he had taigl'd ;
But, wi' his merchandizing load,
Come weel, come wae, he took the road.
Now clouds drave o'er the fields like drift,
Night flung her black cleuk o'er the lift ;
And through the naked trees and hedges,
The horrid storm redoubled rages ;
And, to complete his piteous case,
It blew directly in his face.
Whiles 'gainst the footpath stabs he thump'd,
Whiles o'er the coots in holes he plump'd ;
But on he gae'd, and on he waded,
Till he at length turn'd faint and jaded.
To gang he could nae langer bide,
But lay down by the bare dyke-side.—
Now, wife an' bairns rush'd on his soul,
He groan'd—poor Towser loud did howl ;
And, mourning, cower'd down beside him,
But, oh ! his master couldna heed him,

For now his senses 'gan to dozen,
His vera life-streams maist were frozen,
An't seem'd as if the cruel skies
Exulted o'er their sacrifice ;
For fierce the winds did o'er him hiss,
And dash'd the sleet on his cauld face.
    As on a rock, far, far frae land,
Twa shipwreck'd sailors shiv'ring stand,
If chance a vessel they descry,
Their hearts exult with instant joy ;
Sae was poor Towser joy'd to hear
The tread of trav'llers drawing near ;
He ran, and yowl'd, and fawn'd upon 'em,
But couldna make them understand him.
Till, tugging at the foremost's coat,
He led them to the mournfu' spot,
Where, cauld and stiff, his master lay,
To the rude storm a helpless prey.
    With Caledonian sympathy
They bore him kindly on the way,
Until they reached a cottage bien :
They tauld the case, were welcom'd in.
The rousing fire, the cordial drop,
Restor'd him soon to life and hope :
Fond raptures beam'd in Towser's eye,
And antic gambols spake his joy.
    Wha reads this simple tale may see
The worth of sensibility,
And learn frae it to be humane—
In Towser's life he sav'd his ain.

Baudrons and the Hen-Bird:

A FABLE.

SOME folks there are of such behaviour,
They'll cringe themselves into your favour,
And when you think their friendship staunch is,
They'll tear your character to inches :
T' enforce this truth as well's I'm able,
Please, reader, to peruse a fable.

Deborah, an auld wealthy maiden,
With spleen, remorse, and scandal laden,
Sought out a solitary spat,
To live in quiet with her cat,
A meikle, sonsy, tabby she ane,
(For Deborah abhorr'd a he ane);
And in the house, to be a third,
She gat a wee hen chuckie bird.

Soon as our slee nocturnal ranger,
Beheld the wee bit timid stranger,
She thus began, with friendly fraise :
"Come ben, puir thing, and warm your taes :
This weather's cauld, an' wet, an' dreary,
I'm wae to see you look sae eerie.
Sirs ! how your tail and wings are dreeping,
Ye've surely been in piteous keeping ;
See, here's my dish, come tak' a pick' o't,
But, 'deed, I fear there's scarce a lick o't."

Sic sympathizing words of sense,
Soon gained poor chuckie's confidence ;
And while Deborah mools some crumbs,
Auld baudrons sits, and croodling thrums :
In short, the twa soon grew sae pack,
Chuck roosted upon pussie's back !

But ere sax wee short days were gane,
When baith left in the house alane,
Then thinks the hypocritic sinner,
Now, now's my time to ha'e a dinner :
Sae, with a squat, a spring, and squall,
She tore poor chuckie spawl frae spawl.

Then mind this maxim : rash acquaintance
Aft leads to ruin and repentance.

•

—————

The Ambitious Mite:

A FABLE.

WHEN hope persuades, and fame inspires us,
And pride with warm ambition fires us,
Let reason instant seize the bridle,
And wrest us frae the passions' guidal ;

Else, like the hero of our fable,
We'll aft be plung'd into a habble.
  'Twas on a bonnie simmer day,
When a' the insect tribes were gay,
Some journeying o'er the leaves of roses,
Some brushing thrang their wings and noses,
Some wallowing sweet in bramble blossom,
In luxury's saft downy bosom ;
While ithers of a lower order,
Were perch'd on plantain leaf's smooth border,
Wha frae their twa-inch steeps look'd down,
And viewed the kintra far around.
  Ae pridefu' elf amang the rest,
Wha's pin-point heart bumpt 'gainst his breast
To work some mighty deed of fame,
That would immortalize his name ;
Through future hours would hand him down,
The wonder of an afternoon.
(For ae short day with them appears,
As lang's our lengthened hunder years).
  By chance, at hand, a bow'd horse-hair
Stood up six inches high in air
He plann'd to climb this lofty arch,
With philosophic, deep research
To prove (which aft perplex their heads)
What people peopled ither blades,
Or from keen observation, show,
Whether they peopled were, or no.
  Our tiny hero onward hies,
Quite big with daring enterprise ;
Ascends the hair's curvatured side,
Now pale with fear, now red with pride,
Now hanging pendulous by the claw,
Now glad at having 'scaped a fa' :
What horrid dangers he came through,
Would trifling seem for man to know ;
Suffice, at length he reached the top,
The summit of his pride and hope,
And on his elevated station,
Had plac'd himself for observation,
When, puff—the wind did end the matter,
And dash'd him in a horse-hoof gutter.

Sae let the lesson gi'en us here,
Keep each within his proper sphere;
And when our fancies tak' their flight,
Think on the wee ambitious mite.

The Storm.

WRITTEN IN OCTOBER.

WHILST the dark rains of autumn discolour the brook,
    And the rough winds of winter the woodlands deform;
Here, lonely, I lean by the sheltering rock,
    A-list'ning the voice of the loud howling storm.

Now dreadfully furious it roars on the hill,
    The deep-groaning rocks seem all writhing with pain:
Now awfully calm, for a moment 'tis still,
    Then bursting, it howls and it thunders again.

How cheerless and desert the fields now appear,
    Which so lately in summer's rich verdure were seen,
And each sad drooping spray from its heart drops a tear,
    As seeming to weep its lost mantle of green!

See, beneath the rude wall of yon ruinous pile,
    From the merciless tempest the cattle have fled;
And yon poor patient steed, at the gate by the stile,
    Looks wistfully home for his sheltering shed.

Ah! who would not feel for yon poor gipsy race,
    Peeping out from the door of the old roofless barn?
There my wandering fancy her fortunes might trace,
    And sour Discontent there a lesson might learn.

Yet oft in my bosom arises the sigh,
    That prompts the warm wish distant scenes to explore,
Hope gilds the fair prospect with visions of joy,
    That happiness reigns on some far distant shore.

But yon gray hermit-tree which stood lone on the moor,
    By the fierce driving blast to the earth is blown down;
So the lone, houseless wanderer, unheeded and poor,
    May fall unprotected, unpitied, unknown.

See ! o'er the gray steep, down the deep craggy glen,
  Pours the brown foaming torrent, swelled big with the rain :
It roars through the caves of its dark wizard den,
  Then headlong, impetuous, it sweeps through the plain.

Now the dark heavy clouds have unbosomed their stores,
  And far to the westward the welkin is blue ;
The sullen winds hiss as they die on the moors,
  And the sun faintly shines on yon bleak mountain's brow.

The Resolve.

" Him who ne'er listen'd to the voice of praise,
  The silence of neglect can ne'er appal."--BEATTIE.

'TWAS on a sunny Sabbath-day,
When wark-worn bodies get their play,
I wandered out with serious look,
To read twa page on Nature's book ;
For lang I've thought as little harm in
Hearing a lively out-field sermon,
Even though rowted by a stirk,
As that aft bawl'd in crowded kirk,
By some proud, stern, polemic wight,
Wha cries, " My way alone is right !"
Wha lairs himself in controversy,
Then damns his neighbours without mercy ;
As if the fewer that were spar'd
These few would be the better ser'd.
Now to my tale, digression o'er,
I wandered out by Stanley tow'r :
The lang grass on its tap did wave,
Like weeds upon a warrior's grave ;
Whilk seem'd to mock the bloody braggers,
And grow on theirs as rank's on beggars—
But hold, I'm frae the point again,
I wandered up Gleniffer glen ;
There, leaning 'gainst a mossy rock,
I, musing, eyed the passing brook,
That in its murmurs seemed to say—

" 'Tis thus thy life glides fast away ;
Observe the bubbles on my stream,
Like them, fame is an empty dream ;
They blink a moment to the sun
Then burst, and are for ever gone.
So fame's a bubble of the mind ;
Possess'd, tis nought but empty wind :
No courtly gem e'er purchased dearer,
And ne'er can satisfy the wearer.
Let them wha ha'e a blazing share o't
Confess the truth, they sigh for mair o't
Then let contentment be thy cheer,
And never soar aboon thy sphere ;
Rude storms assail the mountain's brow
That lightly skiff the vale below."
   A gaudy rose was growing near,
Proud tow'ring on its leafy brier,
In fancy's ear it seemed to say—
" Sir, have you seen a flow'r so gay ?
The poets in my praise combine,
Comparing Chloe's charms to mine ;
The sunbeams for my favour sue me,
And dark-browed Night comes down to woo me ;
But when I shrink from his request,
He draps his tears upon my breast,
And in his misty cloud sits wae,
Till chas'd away by rival day.
That streamlet's grov'lling grunting fires me,
Since no ane sees me, but admires me.
See you bit violet 'neath my view,
Wee sallow thing, its nose is blue !
And that bit primrose 'side the breckan,
Poor yellow ghaist, it seems forsaken !
The sun ne'er throws ae transient glow,
Unless when passing whether or no ;
But wisely spurning ane sae mean,
He blinks on me frae morn till e'en."
   To which the primrose calm replied :
" Poor gaudy gowk, suppress your pride,
For soon the strong flow'r-sweeping blast
Shall strew your honours in the dust ;
While I beneath my lowly bield,

Will live and bloom, frae harm concealed :
And while the heavy rain-drops pelt you,
Ye'll maybe think on what I've tell't you."
The rose derisive seemed to sneer,
And waved upon its bonnie brier.
　　Now dark'ning clouds begin to gather,
Presaging sudden change of weather ;
I wander'd hame by Stanley green,
Deep pondering what I'd heard and seen ;
Firmly resolv'd to shun from hence,
The dangerous steeps of eminence :
To drop this rhyming trade for ever,
And creep through life, a plain, day-plodding weaver.

The Parnassiad.

A VISIONARY VIEW.

Come, Fancy, thou hast ever been,
In life's low vale, my ready frien',
　　To cheer the clouded hour ;
Though unfledged with scholastic law,
Some visionary picture draw,
　　With all thy magic pow'r ;
Now to the intellectual eye
　　The glowing prospects rise,
Parnassus' lofty summits high,
　　Far tow'ring 'mid the skies :
　　　　Where vernally, eternally,
　　　Rich leafy laurels grow,
　　　With bloomy bays, through endless days,
　　　　To crown the Poet's brow.

Sure bold is he who dares to climb
Yon awful jutting rock sublime,
　　Who dares Pegasus sit ;
For should brain-ballast prove too light,
He'll spurn him from his airy height,
　　Down to oblivion's pit ;

There, to disgrace for ever doom'd,
　To mourn his sick'ning woes,
And weep that ever he presum'd
　Above the vale of prose.
　　Then, oh beware! with prudent care,
　　　Nor tempt the steeps of fame,
　　And leave behind thy peace of mind,
　　　To gain a sounding name.*

Behold!—yon ready-rhyming carl,
Wi' flatt'ry fir'd, attracts the warl',
By canker'd pers'nal satire;
He takes th' unthinking crowd's acclaim
For sterling proofs of lasting fame,
　And deals his inky spatter.
Now see, he on Pegasus flies,
　With bluff important straddle!
He bears him midway up the skies:
　See, see, he's off the saddle!
　　He headlong tumbles, growls and grumbles,
　　　Down the dark abyss;
　　The noisy core that prais'd before,
　　　Now joins the general hiss.

And see another vent'rer rise,
Deep fraught with fulsome eulogies,
　To win his patron's favour;
One of those adulating things,
That, dangling in the train of kings,
　Give guilt a splendid cover.
He mounts, well prefaced by my lord,
　Inflicts the spur's sharp wound;
Pegasus spurns the great man's word,
　And won't move from the ground.
　　Now mark his face flush'd with disgrace,
　　　Through future life to grieve on;
　　His wishes crost, his hopes all lost,
　　　He sinks into oblivion.

* "The career of genius is rarely that of fortune, and often that of
contempt: even in its most flattering aspect, what is it but plucking a
few brilliant flowers from precipices, while the reward terminates in
honour."—D'ISRAELI.

Yon city scribbler thinks to scale
The cliffs of fame with pastoral,
    In worth, thinks none e'er richer ;
Yet never climb'd the upland steep,
Nor e'er beheld a flock of sheep,
    Save those driven by the butcher ;
Nor e'er marked the gurgling stream,
    Except the common sewer,
On rainy days when dirt and slime
    Pour'd turbid past his door.
        Choice epithets in store he gets
            From Virgil, Shenstone, Pope,
        With tailor art tacks part to part,
        And makes his pastoral up.

But see, rich clad in native worth,
Yon Bard of Nature ventures forth,
    With simple modest tale ;
Applauding millions catch the song,
The raptur'd rocks the notes prolong,
    And hand them to the gale ;
Pegasus kneels—he takes his seat—
    Now see—aloft he tow'rs,
To place him 'bove the reach of fate,
    In Fame's ambrosial bow'rs ;
        To be enroll'd with bards of old,
            In ever-honour'd station ;
        The gods, well-pleas'd, see mortals rais'd
        Worthy of their creation.

Now mark what crowds of hackney scribblers,
Imitators, rhyming dabblers,
    Still follow in the rear !
Pegasus spurns us one by one,
Yet still, fame-struck, we follow on,
    And tempt our fate severe :
In many a dogg'rel epitaph,
    And short-lin'd mournful ditty,
Our " Ahs !—Alases !" raise the laugh,
    Revert the tide of pity :
        Yet still we write in nature's spite,
        Our last piece aye the best ;

Arraigning still, complaining still,
The world for want of taste! *

Observe yon poor deluded man,
With thread-bare coat and visage wan,
Ambitious of a name;
The nat'ral claims of meat and cleeding,
He reckons these not worth the heeding,
But presses on for fame!
The public voice, touchstone of worth,
Anonymous he cries.
But draws the critic's vengeance forth—
His fancied glory dies;
Neglected now, dejected now,
He gives his spleen full scope;
In solitude he chews his cud,
A downright misanthrope.

Then, brother rhymsters, oh beware!
Nor tempt unscar'd the specious snare,
Which self-love often weaves;
Nor doat, with a fond father's pains,
Upon the offspring of your brains,
For fancy oft deceives:
To lighten life, a wee bit sang
Is sure a sweet illusion!
But ne'er provoke the critic's stang,
By premature intrusion:
Lock up your piece, let fondness cease,
Till mem'ry fail to bear it,
With critic lore then read it o'er,
Yourself may judge its merit.

Connel and Flora:
A SCOTTISH LEGEND.

"THE western sun shines o'er the loch,
And gilds the mountain's brow,
But what are Nature's smiles to me,
Without the smile of you?

* "Still restless fancy drives us headlong on;
With dreams of wealth, and friends, and laurels won,
On ruin's brink we sleep, and wake undone."—AUTHOR.

Oh, will ye go to Garnock side,
   Where birks and woodbines twine :
I've sought you oft to be my bride,
   When, when will you be mine ?"

" Oft as ye sought me for your bride,
   My mind spoke frae my e'e ;
Then wherefore seek to win a heart
   That is not mine to gi'e ?

With Connel, down the dusky dale,
   Long plighted are my vows ;
He won my heart before I wist
   I had a heart to lose."

The fire flash'd from his eyes of wrath,
   Dark gloom'd his heavy brow,
He grasped her in his arms of strength,
   And strain'd to lay her low.

She wept and cried—the rocks replied :
   The echoes from their cell,
On fairy wing, swift bore her voice
   To Connel of the dell.

With vengeful haste he hied him up ;
   But when stern Donald saw
The youth approach, deep-stung with guilt,
   He shame-fac'd fled awa'.

"Ah ! stay, my Connel—sheath thy sword ;
   Oh, do not him pursue !
For mighty are his arms of strength,
   And thou the fight may'st rue."

" No ! wait thou here—I'll soon return :
   I mark'd him from the wood ;
The lion heart of jealous love
   Burns for its rival's blood.

Ho ! stop thee, coward !—villain vile !
   With all thy boasted art,
My sword's blade soon shall dim its shine
   Within thy reynard heart."

" Ha ! foolish stripling, dost thou urge
    The deadly fight with me ?
This arm strove hard in Flodden field,
    Dost think 'twill shrink from thee ?"

" Thy frequent vaunts of Flodden field,
    Were ever fraught with guile ;
For honour ever marks the brave,
    But thou'rt a villain vile !"

Their broad blades glitter to the sun,
    The woods resound each clash,
Young Connel sinks 'neath Donald's sword,
    With deep and deadly gash.

" Ah ! dearest Flora, soon our morn
    Of love is overcast !
The hills look dim ; alas ! my love !"
    He groaned—and breathed his last.

" Stay, ruthless ruffian ! murderer !
    Here glut thy savage wrath !
Be thou the baneful minister
    To join us low in death !"

In wild despair she tore her hair,
    Sunk speechless by his side :
Mild evening wept in dewy tears,
    And, wrapt in night, she died.

The Cock-pit.

The barbarous amusement of seeing two animals instinctively destroying
each other, certainly affords sufficient scope for the pen of the satirist
The author thought he could not do it more effectually than by giving
a picture of the cock-pit, and describing a few of the characters who
generally may be seen at such glorious contests.

" THE great, the important hour is come,
    Oh, hope ! thou wily nurse ;
See bad luck behind thy back,
    Dark-breeding, deep remorse."

No fancied muse will I invoke
    To grace my humble strain,
But sing my song in homely phrase,
    Inspir'd by what I've seen.

Here comes a feeder with his charge,
    'Mong friends 'tis whisper'd straight,
How long he swung him on a string,
    To bring him to his weight.

The carpet's laid—pit money drawn—
    All's high with expectation ;
With bird's bereft of Nature's garb,
    The " handlers" take their station.

What roaring, betting, bawling, swearing,
    Now assail the ear !
" Three pounds!—four pounds on Philips' cock,
    —Done ! done, by G—d, sir, here !"

Now cast a serious eye around—
    Behold the motley group,
All gamblers, swindlers, ragamuffins,
    Votaries of the stoup.

Here sits a wretch with meagre face,
    And sullen drowsy eye ;
Nor speaks he much—last night, at cards,
    A gamester drain'd him dry.

Here bawls another vent'rous soul,
    Who risks his every farthing ;
What de'il's the matter ! though at home
    His wife and brats are starving.

See, here's a father 'gainst a son,
    A brother 'gainst a brother ;
Who e'en with more than common spite,
    Bark hard at one another !

But see yon fellow all in black,
    His looks speak inward joy ;
Mad happy since his father's deat'
    Sporting his legacy.

And, mark—that aged debauchee,
  With red bepimpl'd face—
He fain would bet a crown or two,
  But purse is not in case.

But hark, that cry !—"He's run, he's run !"—
  And loud huzzas take place—
Now mark what deep dejection sits
  On every loser's face.

Observe the owner—frantic man,
  With imprecations dread,
    He grasps his vanquish'd idol-god,
    And twirls off his head.

But, bliss attend their feeling souls,
  Who no such deeds delight in !
Brutes are but brutes, let men be men,
  Nor pleasure in cock-fighting.

———

Prologue to the Gentle Shepherd :

SPOKEN IN A PROVINCIAL THEATRE.

YE patronizers of our little party,
My heart's e'en light to see you a' sae hearty,
I'm fain indeed, and troth ! I've meikle cause,
Since your blithe faces half insure applause.
We come this night wi' nae new-fangl'd story,
Of knave's deceit, or fop's vain blust'ring glory,
Nor harlequin's wild pranks, with skin like leopard,—
We're come to gi'e your ain auld Gentle Shepherd,
Whilk aye will charm, and will be read, and acket,
Till Time himsel' turn auld, and kick the bucket.
I mind, langsyne, when I was just a callan,
That a' the kintra rang in praise o' Allan ;
Ilk rising generation toots his fame,
And, hun'er years to come, 'twill be the same :
For wha has read, though e'er sae lang sinsyne
But keeps the living picture on his min',
Approves bauld Patie's clever manly turn,
And maist thinks Roger cheap o' Jenny's scorn ;
His dowless gait, the cause of a' his care,

K

For " nane except the brave, deserve the fair."
Hence sweet young Peggy lo'ed her manly Pate,
And Jenny geck'd at Roger, dowf and blate.
   Our gude Sir William stands a lesson leal
To lairds wha'd ha'e their vassals lo'e them weel ;
To prince and peer, this maxim it imparts,
Their greatest treasures are the people's hearts.
   Frae Glaud and Simon would we draw a moral,
" The virtuous youth-time mak's the canty carl ;"
The twa auld birkies caper blithe and bauld,
Nor shaw the least regret that they're turn'd auld.
   Poor Bauldy ! oh, 'tis like to split my jaws !
I think I see him under Madge's claws :
Sae may Misfortune tear him spawl and plack,
Wha'd wrang a bonnie lassie, and syne draw back.
   But sirs, to you I maist forgat my mission ;
I'm sent to beg a truce to criticism :
We don't pretend to speak by square and rule,
Like you wise chaps bred up in Thespian school ;
And to your wishes should we not succeed,
Pray be sae kind as tak' the will for deed.

The Contrast.

INSCRIBED TO JAMES SCADLOCK.—AUGUST, 1803.

WHEN Love proves false, and friends betray us,
All nature seems a dismal chaos
   Of wretchedness and woe ;
We stamp mankind a base ingrate,
Half loathing life, we challenge fate
   To strike the final blow.
     Then settled grief, with wild despair,
      Stares from our blood-shot eyes,
     Though oft we try to hide our care,
      And check our bursting sighs,
       Still vexed, sae wretched,
        We seek some lonely wood,
       There sighing, and crying,
        We pour the briny flood.

The contrast mark—what joys we find,
With friends sincere and beauty kind,
    Congenial to our wishes ;
Then life appears a summer's day,
Adown Time's crystal stream we play,
    As sportive's little fishes.
        We see nought then but general good,
            Which warm pervades all nature ;
        Our hearts expand with gratitude
            Unto the great Creator.
                Then let's revere the virtuous fair,
                    The friend whose truth is tried,
                For, without these, go where we please,
                    We'll always find a void.

Ode to Jealousy.

MARK what demon hither bends,
Gnawing still his finger ends,
Wrapt in contemplation deep,
Wrathful, yet inclin'd to weep.

Thy wizard gait, thy breath-check'd broken sigh,
Thy burning cheeks, thy lips, black, wither'd, dry ;
Thy side-thrown glance, with wild malignant eye,
Betray thy foul intent, infernal Jealousy.

    Hence, thou self-tormenting fiend,
    To thy spleen-dug cave descend ;
    Fancying wrongs that never were,
    Rend thy bosom, tear thy hair,
    Brood fell hate within thy den,
    Come not near the haunts of men.

Let man be faithful to his brother man,
Nor, guileful, still pervert kind Heaven's plan ;
Then slavish fear, and mean distrust shall cease,
And confidence confirm a lasting mental peace.

The Trifler's Sabbath-Day.

Loud sounds the deep-mouthed parish bell,
  Religion kirkward hies,
John lies in bed and counts each knell,
  And thinks 'tis time to rise.

But, oh how weak are man's resolves!
  His projects ill to keep,
John thrusts his nose beneath the clothes,
  And dozes o'er asleep.

Now fairy fancy plays her freaks
  Upon his sleep-swell'd brain;
He dreams—he starts—he mutt'ring speaks,
  And waukens wi' a grane.

He rubs his een—the clock strikes Twelve—
  Impell'd by hunger's gripe,
One mighty effort backs resolve—
  He's up—at last he's up!

Hunger appeased, his cutty pipe
  Employs his time till Two,—
And now he saunters through the house,
  And knows not what to do.

He baits the trap—catches a mouse—
  He sports it round the floor;
He swims it in a water tub—
  Gets glorious fun till Four!

And now of cats, and mice, and rats,
  He tells a thousand tricks,
Till even dullness tires himself,
  For, hark—the clock strikes Six!

Now view him in his easy chair
  Recline his pond'rous head;
'Tis Eight—now Bessie rakes the fire,
  And John must go to bed!

Ode,

IN IMITATION OF PETER PINDAR (DR. WALCOTT).

THE simile's a very useful thing ;
  This, priests and poets needs must own ;
  For when the clockwork of their brains runs down,
A simile winds up the mental spring.
  For instance, when a priest does scan
      The fall of man,
  And all its consequences dire,
He makes him first a little sportive pig,
So clean, so innocent, so trig,
  And then, an aged sow, deep wallowing in the mire!
      Yes, sure the simile's a useful thing,
      Another instance I will bring.
Thou'st seen a cork tost on the rain-swell'd stream,
Now, up, now down, now whirl'd round and round,
      Yet still 'twould swim,
And all the torrent's fury could not drown't :
  So have I seen a forward empty fop
  Tost in Wit's blanket, ridicul'd, et cetera ;
  Yet, after all the banter, off he'd hop,
Quite confident in self-sufficiency.
      Ah! had kind Heaven,
      For a defence,
  Allow'd me half the brazen confidence
That she to many a cork-brain'd fool had given!

The Portrait of Guilt:

IN IMITATION OF M. G. LEWIS.

'TWAS night, and the winds through the dark forest roar'd,
From Heaven's wide cat'racts the torrents down pour'd,
  And blue lightnings flash'd on the eye ;
Demoniac howlings were heard in the air,
With groans of deep anguish, and shrieks of despair,
  And hoarse thunders growl'd through the sky.

Pale, breathless, and trembling the dark villain stood,
His hands and his clothes all bespotted with blood,
   His eyes wild with terror did stare;
The earth yawn'd around him, and sulphurous blue,
From the flame-boiling gaps, did expose to his view,
   A gibbet and skeleton bare.

With horror he shrunk from a prospect so dread,
The blast swung the clanking chains over his head,
   The rattling bones sung in the wind;
The lone bird of night from the abbey did cry,
He looked o'er his shoulder intending to fly,
   But a spectre stood ghastly behind.

"Stop, deep hell-taught villain!" the ghost did exclaim,
"With thy brother of guilt here to expiate thy crime,
   And atone for thy treacherous vow:
'Tis here thou shalt hang to the vultures a prey,
Till piece-meal they tear thee and bear thee away,
   And thy bones rot unburied below."

Now closing all round him fierce demons did throng,
In sounds all unholy they howl'd their death-song,
   And the vultures around them did scream;
Now clenching their claws in his fear-bristled hair,
Loud yelling they bore him aloft in the air,
   And the murd'rer awoke—'twas a dream.

The Hauntet Wud:

IN IMITATION OF JOHN BARBOUR.

Quhy screim the crowis owr yonder wud,
   With loude and clamourynge dynne,
Haf deifenynge the torrentis roar,
   Quhilk dashis owr yon linne?

Quhy straye the flokis far outowr,
   Alang the stanery lee,
And wil nocht graze anear the wud,
   Thof ryche the pasturis be?

And quhy dis oft the sheipherdis dog,
  Gif that ane lamikyne strayc,
Ayc yamf and yowl bcsyde the wud,
  Nae farther yn wil gayc?

" Marvil thee nocht at quhat thou scist,"
  The tremblynge rusticke sayde.
" For yn that feindis-hauntet wud,
  Hath guyltlesse blude been sched.

" Thou scist far down yon buschyc howe,
  An eldrin castil greyc,
With teth of tyme, and weir of wyndis,
  Fast mould'ryng yn decayc.

" 'Twas thair the jealous Barronne livit,
  With Ladie Anne hys wyfe;
He fleichit her neath that wudis dark glume,
  And revit her ther of lyffe.

" And eir hyr fayre bodyc was found,
  The flesch cam frac the banc,
The snailis sat feistyng onne hyr cheikis.
  The spydiris velit hyr ein.

" And evir synce nae beist nor byrde
  Will byde twa nichtis thair,
For fearful yellis and screichis wylde
  Are heird throuch nicht sae dreir."

Ode.

WRITTEN FOR, AND READ AT THE CELEBRATION OF ROBERT BURNS
BIRTH-DAY, BY THE PAISLEY BURNS' CLUB, 1805.

ONCE on a time, almighty Jove
Invited all the minor gods above,
To spend one day in social festive pleasure:
  His legal robes were laid aside,
  His crown, his sceptre, and his pride;
      And wing'd with joy,
      The hours did fly,
The happiest ever Time did measure.

Of love and social harmony they sung,
Till heav'n's high golden arches echoing rung;
And as they quaff'd the nectar-flowing can,
　　　　Their toast was,
"Universal peace 'twixt man and man."

Their godships' eyes beam'd gladness with the wish,
And Mars half-redden'd with a guilty blush;
Jove swore he'd hurl each rascal to perdition,
Who'd dare deface his works with wild ambition;
But pour'd encomiums on each patriot band,
Who, hating conquest, guard their native land.

Loud thund'ring plaudits shook the bright abodes,
Till Merc'ry, solemn-voiced, assail'd their ears,
Informing, that a stranger, all in tears,
Weeping, implored an audience of the gods.
Jove, ever prone to succour the distrest,
A swell redressive glow'd within his breast,
He pitied much the stranger's sad condition,
And ordered his immediate admission.

The stranger enter'd, bow'd respect to all,
Respectful silence reign'd throughout the hall:
His chequer'd robes excited their surprise,
Richly transvers'd with various glowing dyes;
A target on his strong left arm he bore,
Broad as the shield the mighty Fingal wore;
The glowing landscape on its centre shin'd,
And massy thistles round the borders twin'd;
His brows were bound with yellow-blossom'd broom,
Green birch and roses blending in perfume;
His eyes beam'd honour, though all red with grief,
And thus heaven's King spake comfort to the chief:
"My son, let speech unfold thy cause of woe,
Say, why does melancholy cloud thy brow?
'Tis mine the wrongs of virtue to redress;
Speak, for 'tis mine to succour deep distress."

Then thus he spake: "O King! by thy command,
I am the guardian of that far-fam'd land
Nam'd Caledonia, great in arts and arms,
And every worth that social fondness charms,

With every virtue that the heart approves,
Warm in their friendships, rapt'rous in their loves,
Profusely generous, obstinately just,
Inflexible as death their vows of trust ;
For independence fires their noble minds,
Scorning deceit, as gods do scorn the fiends.
But what avail the virtues of the North,
No patriot bard to celebrate their worth,
No heav'n-taught mistrel, with the voice of song,
To hymn their deeds, and make their names live long ?
And ah ! should Luxury, with soft winning wiles,
Spread her contagion o'er my subject isles,
My hardy sons, no longer Valour's boast,
Would sink despis'd, their wonted greatness lost.
Forgive my wish, O King ! I speak with awe,
Thy will is fate, thy word is sovereign law !
Oh ! would'st thou deign thy suppliant to regard,
And grant my country one true patriot bard,
My sons would glory in the blessing given,
And virtuous deeds spring from the gift of Heaven !"

To which the god : " My son, cease to deplore,
Thy name in song shall sound the world all o'er ;
Thy bard shall rise, full fraught with all the fire
That Heav'n and free-born nature can inspire :
Ye sacred Nine, your golden harps prepare,
T' instruct the fav'rite of my special care,
That whether the song be rais'd to war or love,
His soul-wing'd strains may equal those above.
Now faithful to thy trust, from sorrow free,
Go wait the issue of our high degree."—
Speechless the Genius stood, in glad surprise,
Adorning gratitude beam'd in his eyes ;
The promis'd bard his soul with transport fills,
And light with joy he sought his native hills.

'Twas from regard to Wallace and his worth,
Jove honour'd Coila with his birth ;
     And on that morn,
     When Burns was born,
     Each Muse with joy,
     Did hail the boy ;

And Fame, on tiptoe, fain would blown her horn,
But Fate forbade the blast, so premature,
Till worth should sanction it beyond the critic's power.
His merits proven—Fame her blast hath blown,
Now Scotia's Bard o'er all the world is known —
But trembling doubts here check my unpolished lays,
What can they add to a whole world's praise ?
Yet, while revolving time this day returns,
Let Scotsmen glory in the name of BURNS.

Ode,

WRITTEN FOR, AND PERFORMED AT THE CELEBRATION OF BURNS
BIRTH-DAY, BY THE PAISLEY BURNS' CLUB, 1807.

RECITATIVE.

WHILE Gallia's chief, with cruel conquests vain,
Bids clanging trumpets rend the skies,
The widow's, orphan's, and the father's sighs,
I breathe, hissing through the guilty strain;
Mild Pity hears the harrowing tones,
Mix'd with shrieks and dying groans ;
While warm Humanity, afar,
Weeps o'er the ravages of war,
And shudd'ring hears Ambition's servile train,
Rejoicing o'er their thousands slain.
But when the song to worth is given,
The grateful anthem wings its way to heaven:
Rings through the mansions of the bright abodes,
And melts to ecstasy the list'ning gods :
          Apollo, on fire,
          Strikes with rapture the lyre,
        And the Muses the summons obey ;
          Joy wings the glad sound,
          To the world's around,
        Till all nature re-echoes the lay.—
Then raise the song, ye vocal few,
Give the praise to merit due.

SONG.

Though dark scowling Winter, in dismal array,
  Remarshals his storms on the bleak hoary hill,
With joy we assemble to hail the great day
  That gave birth to the Bard who ennobles our isle:
Then loud to his merits the song let us raise,
  Let each true Caledonian exult in his praise;
For the glory of genius, its dearest reward,
  Is the laurel entwin'd by his country's regard.

Let the Muse bring fresh honours his name to adorn,
  Let the voice of glad melody pride in the theme,
For the genius of Scotia, in ages unborn,
  Will light up her torch at the blaze of his fame.
When the dark mist of ages lies turbid between,
Still his star of renown through the gloom shall be seen,
And his rich blooming laurels, so dear to the Bard,
Will be cherish'd for aye by his country's regard.

RECITATIVE.

Yes, BURNS, " thou dear departed shade !"
When rolling centuries have fled,
Thy name shall still survive the wreck of time,
Shall rouse the genius of thy native clime;
Bards yet unborn, and patriots shall come,
And catch fresh ardour at thy hallow'd tomb !
There's not a cairn-built cottage on our hills,
  Nor rural hamlet on our fertile plains,
  But echoes to the magic of thy strains,
While every heart with highest transport thrills.
Our country's melodies shall perish never,
For, BURNS, thy songs shall live for ever,
  Then, once again, ye vocal few,
  Give the song o merit due.

SONG,

Hail, ye glorious sons of song,
  Who wrote to humanize the soul!
To you our highest strains belong,
  Your names shall crown our friendly bowl:
    But chiefly BURNS, above the rest,
      We dedicate this night to thee;
    Engrav'd in every Scotsman's breast,
      Thy name, thy worth, shall ever be!

Fathers of our country's weal,
  Sternly virtuous, bold and free?
Ye taught your sons to fight, yet feel
  The dictates of humanity:

But chiefly, BURNS, above the rest,
　We dedicate this night to thee ;
Engrav'd in every Scotsman's breast,
　Thy name, thy worth, shall ever be!

Haughty Gallia threats our coast,
　We hear her vaunts with disregard,
Secure in valour, still we boast
　"The Patriot, and the Patriot-bard."
But, chiefly, BURNS, above the rest,
　We dedicate this night to thee :
Engrav'd in every Scotsman's breast,
　Thy name, thy worth, shall ever be!

Yes, Caledonians! to our country true,
Which Danes nor Romans never could subdue,
Firmly resolv'd our native rights to guard,
Let's toast "The Patriot, and the Patriot-bard."

Ode,

RECITED BY THE PRESIDENT AT THE CELEBRATION OF BURNS' BIRTH-DAY,
BY THE PAISLEY BURNS' CLUB, 1810.

AGAIN the happy day returns,
A day to Scotsmen ever dear ;
Though bleakest of the changeful year,
　It blest us with a BURNS.

　Fierce the whirling blast may blow,
Drifting wide the crispy snow ;
Rude the ruthless storms may sweep,
Howling round our mountains steep,
While the heavy lashing rains,
Swell our rivers, drench our plains,
And the angry ocean roars
Round our broken, craggy shores ;
But mindful of our poet's worth,
We hail the honour'd day that gave him birth.

　Come, ye vot'ries of the lyre,
Trim the torch of heav'nly fire,
Raise the song in Scotia's praise,
Sing anew her bonnie braes,
Sing her thousand siller streams,

Bickering to the sunny beams;
Sing her sons beyond compare,
Sing her dochters, peerless, fair;
Sing, till winter's storms be o'er,
The matchless bards that sung before;
And I, the meanest of the Muse's train,
Shall join my feeble aid to swell the strain.

Dear Scotia, though thy clime be cauld,
Thy sons were ever brave and bauld,
Thy dochters modest, kind, and leal,
The fairest in creation's fiel';
Alike inur'd to every toil,
Thou'rt foremost in the battle broil;
Prepar'd alike in peace and weir,
To guid the plough or wield the spear;
As the mountain torrent raves,
Dashing through its rugged caves,
So the Scottish legions pour
Dreadful in the avenging hour;
But when Peace, with kind accord,
Bids them sheath the sated sword,
See them in their native vales,
Jocund as the summer gales,
Cheering labour all the day,
With some merry roundelay.

Dear Scotia, though thy nights be drear,
When surly winter rules the year,
Around thy cottage hearth are seen
The glow of health, the cheerful mien;
The mutual glance that fondly shares,
A neighbour's joys, a neighbour's cares;
Here oft, while raves the wind and weet,
The canty lads and lasses meet.
Sae light of heart, sae full of glee,
Their gaits sae artless and sae free,
The hours of joy come dancing on,
To share their frolic and their fun.
Here many a song and jest goes round
With tales of ghosts and rites profound,
Perform'd in dreary wizard glen,

By wrinkled hags and warlock men,
Or of the hell-fee'd crew combin'd,
Carousing on the midnight wind,
On some infernal errand bent,
While darkness shrouds their black intent ;
But chiefly, BURNS, thy songs delight
To charm the weary winter night,
And bid the lingering moments flee,
Without a care unless for thee,
Wha sang sae sweet and dee't sae soon,
And sought thy native sphere aboon.
"Thy lovely Jean," thy "Nannie, O,"
Thy much lov'd "Caledonia,"
Thy "Wat ye wha's in yonder town,"
Thy "Banks and Braes o' Bonnie Doon,"
Thy "Shepherdess on Afton Braes,"
Thy "Logan Lassie's " bitter waes,
Are a' gane o'er sae sweetly tun'd,
That e'en the storm, pleased with the sound,
Fa's lown and sings with eerie slight,
"O let me in this ae night."
Alas! our best, our dearest Bard,
How poor, how great was his reward ;
Unaided he has fix'd his name,
Immortal, in the rolls of fame ;
    Yet who can hear without a tear,
    What sorrows wrung his manly breast,
To see his little helpless filial band,
Imploring succour from a father's hand,
    And there no succour near?
Himself the while with sick'ning woes opprest,
    Fast hast'ning on to where the weary rest:—
For this let Scotia's bitter tears atone,
She reck'd not half his worth till he was gone.

Prayer, under Affliction.

ALMIGHTY Power, who wing'st the storm,
    And calm'st the raging wind,
Restore health to my wasted form,
    And tranquilize my mind.

For, ah ! how poignant is the grief,
   Which self-misconduct brings,
When racking pains find no relief,
   And injur'd conscience stings.

Let penitence forgiveness plead,
   Hear lenient mercy's claims,
Thy justice let be satisfied,
   And blotted out my crimes.

But should thy sacred law of right,
   Seek life a sacrifice,
Oh ! haste that awful, solemn night
   When death shall veil mine eyes.

The Poor Bowlman's Remonstrance.

THROUGH winter's cold and summer's heat,
I earn my scanty fare ;
From morn till night, along the street,
   I cry my earthen ware :
Then, oh let pity sway your souls !
   And mock not that decrepitude,
   Which draws me from my solitude,
To cry my plates and bowls !

From thoughtless youth I often brook
   The trick and taunt of scorn,
And though indiff'rence marks my look,
   My heart with grief is torn :
Then, oh let pity sway your souls !
   Nor sneer contempt in passing by;
   Nor mock, derisive, while I cry,
"Come, buy my plates and bowls."

The potter moulds the passive clay,
   To all the forms you see :
And that same Pow'r that formed you,
   Hath likewise fashion'd me.
Then, oh let pity sway your souls !
   Though needy, poor as poor can be,
   I stoop not to your charity,
But cry my plates and bowls.

The Choice.

YE votaries of pleasure and ease,
　Proud, wasting in riot the day,
Drive on your career as ye please,
　Let me follow a different way.
The woodland, the mountain, and hill,
　With the birds singing sweet from the tree,
The soul with serenity fill,
　And have pleasures more pleasing to me.

When I see you parade through the streets,
　With affected, unnatural airs,
I smile at your low trifling gaits,
　And could heartily lend you my prayers.
Great Jove! was it ever designed
　That man should his reason lay down,
And barter the peace of his mind
　For the follies and fashions of town?

I'll retire to yon broom-coloured fields,
　On the green mossy turf I'll recline,
The pleasure's that solitude yields,
　Composure and peace shall be mine.
There Thomson or Shenstone I'll read,
　Well pleased with each well-managed theme,
With nothing to trouble my head,
　But ambition to imitate them.

On Invocation.

LET ither bards exhaust their stock
Of heavenly names on heavenly folk,
And gods and goddesses invoke
　　　　To guide the pen,
While, just as well, a barber's block
　　　　Would serve their en'.

Nae muse ha'e I like guid Scotch drink;
It mak's the dormant soul to think,
Gars wit and rhyme thegither clink,
　　　　In canty measure;

And even though half-fu' we wink,
     Inspires wi' pleasure.

Whyles dullness stands for modest merit,
And impudence for manly spirit ;
To ken what worth each does inherit,
     Just try the bottle ;
Send round the glass, and dinna spare it,
     Ye'll see their mettle.

Oh, would the gods but grant my wish,
My constant prayer would be for this :
That love sincere, with health and peace,
     My lot they'd clink in,
With now and then the social joys
     O' friendly drinkin'.

And when youth's rattlin' days are done,
And age brings on life's afternoon,
Then, like a summer setting sun,
     Brightly serene,
Smiling look back, and slidder down,
     To rise again.

The Bacchanalians.

ENCIRCLED in a cloud of smoke
  Sat the convivial core,
Like lightning flashed the merry joke,
  The thundering laugh did roar.
Blythe Bacchus pierced his favourite hoard,
  The sparkling glasses shine :
" 'Tis this," they cry, " come, sweep the board,
Which makes us all divine !"

Apollo tuned the vocal shell,
  With song, with catch, and glee :
The sonorous hall the notes did swell,
  And echoed merrily.

Each sordid, selfish, little thought,
    For shame itself did drown;
And social love, with every draught,
    Approved them for her own.

"Come fill another bumper up,
    And drink in Bacchus' praise,
Who sent the kind, congenial cup,
    Such heavenly joys to raise!"

Great Jove, quite mad to see such fun,
    At Bacchus 'gan to curse,
And to remind they were but men,
    Sent down the fiend Remorse.

Allan's Ale.

Come a ye friendly, social pack,
Wha meet with glee to club your plack,
Attend while I rehearse a fact,
        That winna fail;
Nae drink can raise a canty crack
        Like Allan's ale.

It waukens wit, and makes us merry,
As England's far-famed Canterbury;
Rich wines, frae Lisbon, or Canary;
        Let gentles hail,
But we can be as brisk and airy
        Wi' Allan's ale.

It bears the gree, I'se gi'e my aith,
Of Widow Dean's and Rollston's baith,
Wha may cast by their brewing graith,
        Baith pat and pail,
Since Paisley wisely puts mair faith
        In Allan's ale.

Unlike the poor, sma' penny-wheep,
Whilk worthless, petty change-folk keep,

O'er whilk mirth never deigned to peep,
    Sae sour and stale;
I've seen me joyous frisk and leap
    Wi' Allan's ale.

Whether a social friendly meeting,
Or politicians thrang debating,
Or benders, blessed your wizzens weeting,
    Mark well my tale,
Ye'll find nae drink half worth your getting
    Like's Allan's ale.

When bleak December's blasts do blaw,
And nature's face is co'ered wi' snaw,
Poor bodies scarce do work at a',
    The cauld's sae snell,
But meet and drink their cares awa'
    Wi' Allan's ale.

Let auld Kilmarnock make a fraise,
What she has done in better days,
Her threepenny ance her fame could raise,
    O'er muir and dale,
But Paisley now may claim the praise
    Wi' Allan's ale.

Let selfish wights impose their notions,
And damn the man won't take their lessons,
I scorn their threats, I scorn their cautions,
    Say what they will;
Let friendship crown our best devotions
    Wi' Allan's ale.

While sun, and moon, and stars endure,
And aid wi' light "a random splore,"
Still let each future social core,
    Its praises tell:
Adored aye, and for evermore,
    Be Allan's ale!

Ode for the Anniversary of the Birth of Tannahill.

BY ALEXANDER RODGER.

WHILE certain parties in the state
Meet yearly to commemmorate
The birth of their great "heaven-born" head,
Wha lang did Britain's councils lead,
And, in the face of downright facts,
Launch forth in praise of certain acts,
As deeds of first-rate magnitude,
Performed a' for the public good,
By this rare pink o' politicians,
This matchless prince o' state physicians;
Whose greatest skill in bleeding lay,
Bleeding the state into decay:
For, studying the great Sangrado,
There's little doubt but he got haud o'
The secret of that great man's art,
At which he soon grew most expert:
As his prescriptions, like his master's,
Still ran on lancets more than plasters;
A proper mode, nae doubt, when nations,
Like men are fashed wi' inflammations;
But somewhat dangerous when the patient,
From being rather scrimply rationed,
Has little blood to spare, and when
(With all respects for learned men)
He has much less desire to look
To the physician than the cook.
While thus they meet and yearly dine,
And o'er the flowing cups o' wine,
By studied speech or well-timed toast,
Declare it is their greatest boast,
That they were friends o' that great pilot,
Wha brav'd the storm by his rare skill o't,
And brought the vessel fairly through,
Though mutinous were half the crew.

At then, these Pitt-adoring fellows
Are careful to forget to tell us,
That running foul o' some rude rock,
He gied the vessel such a shock,
As shattered a' her stately hull,
So that her owner, Mr Bull,
So terrible a loss sustaining,
Has ever since been sair complaining.
In fact this once brave, stout, plump fellow,
With face now of a sickly yellow ;
A constitution sadly shattered,
A frame wi' toil and sickness battered
Wearing away by constant wasting,
Down to the grave seems fast a-hasting ;
But yet he vows, if he be spared,
He'll have her thoroughly repaired ;
Nor weary out his gallant crew
By toiling mair than men can do ;
For now it tak's them ceaseless pumping
To keep the crazy hulk from swamping :
Na, trowth, they tell us nought like that,
The're no sae candid, weel I wot,
But getting a' quite pack thegither,
They bandy compliments at ither,
Sae thick and fast, that mutual flatteries
Are playing-off like bomb-shell batteries :
Or rather, to come lower down,
For that's a similie too high flown,
It's somewhat like a boyish yoking
At battledore and shuttlecocking ;
For soon as this one gies his crack,
The next ane's ready to pay back
His fulsome compliments galore ;
And thus is blarney's battledore
Applied to flattery's shuttlecock,
Till ilk ane round gets stroke for stroke.
    A different task is ours indeed ;
We meet to pay the grateful meed—
The meed of just esteem sincere,
To ane whose memory we hold dear ;
To ane whose name demands respect,
Although wi' nae court titles decked ;

To ane wha never learned the gate
Of fawning meanly on the great ;
To ane wha never turned his coat,
To mak' a sinfu' penny o't ;
To ane wha never speeled to favour
By turning mankind's chief enslaver ;
To ane wha never did aspire
To set and keep the world on fire ;
To ane wha ne'er, by mischief brewing,
Raised himsel' on his country's ruin ;
But humbly glided on through life,
Remote from party jars and strife ;
A quite innoffensive man,
As ever life's short racecourse ran ;
A simple, honest child of nature still,—
In short, our ain dear minstrel, Tannahill.
    O Tannahill ! thou bard revered,
Thy name shall ever be endeared
To Scotia, thy loved land of song,
While her pure river's glide along ;
While her bleak rugged mountains high
Point their rude summits to the sky ;
While yellow harvests on her plains
Reward her children's toils and pains ;
And while her sons and daughters leal
The inborn glow of freedom feel,
Her woods, her rocks, her hills and glens,
Shall echo thy delightful strains.
While " Jura's cliff's " are capped with snows,
While the " dark-winding Carron " flows ;
While high " Benlomond " rears his head
To catch the sun's last radiance shed :
While sweet " Gleniffer's dewy dell "
Blooms wi' the " crawflower's early bell ;"
While smiles " Glenkilloch's sunny brae,"
Made classic by thy tender lay ;
While waves the " wood of Craigielee,"
Where " Mary's heart was won by thee ;"
Thy name, thy artless minstrelsy,
Sweet bard of nature, ne'er shall die,
But thou wil't be remembered still,
Meek, unassuming Tannahill.

What though with Burns thou could'st not vie,
In diving deep or soaring high ;
What though thy genius did not blaze,
Like his to draw the public gaze,
Yet thy sweet numbers, free from art,
Like his can touch, can melt the heart,
The laverock may soar till he's lost in the sky,
   Yet the modest wee lintie that sings frae the tree,
Although he aspire not to regions so high,
   His song is as sweet as the laverock's to me :
And oh, thy wild warblings are sweet, Tannahill !
   Whatever thy theme be, love, grief, or despair,
The tones of thy lyre move our feelings at will,
   For nature, all-powerful, predominates there.
But while the bard we eulogize,
Shall we the man neglect to prize ?
No, perish every virtue first,
   And every vice usurp its place ;
With every ill let man be cursed,
   Ere we do ought so mean and base.
Shall bloody warriors fill the rolls of fame,
And niches in her lofty temple claim ?
Shall the unfeeling scourgers of mankind,
To mercy deaf, to their own interest blind ?
Shall the depopulators of the earth,
Without one particle of real worth,
Whose lives are one compounded mass of crime,
Be handed down by fame to latest time,
The admiration of each future age,
They whose vile names are blots on every page !
And shall the child of virtue be forgot,
Because the inmate of an humble cot ?
Shall he whose heart was open, warm, sincere.
Who gave to want his mite, to woe his tear ;
Whose friendship still was steady, warm, and sure ;
Whose love was tender, constant, ardent, pure ;
Whose fine-toned feelings, generous and humane,
Were hurt to give the meanest reptile pain ;
Whose filial love for her who gave him birth
Has seldom found a parallel on earth :
Shall he, forgotten, in oblivion lie ?
Forbid it, every sacred power on high !

Forbid it, every virtue here below.
Shall such a precious gem lie buried? no:
Historians may forget him, if they will,
But age will tell to age the worth of Tannahill.
When mighty conquerors shall be forgot,
When, like themselves, their very name shall rot;
When even the story of their deeds is lost,
Or only heard with horror and disgust;
When happy man, from tyranny set free,
Shall wonder if such things could really be;
And bless his stars that he was not on earth
When such destructive monsters were brought forth;
When the whole human family shall be one,
In every clime below the circling sun;
And every man shall live secure and free,
Beneath his vine, beneath his own fig-tree;
No savage hordes his dwelling to invade,
Nor plunderer, daring to make him afraid;
When things are prized not by their showy dress,
But by the solid worth which they possess;
Even then our much-lamented bard
Those times shall venerate with deep regard;
His songs shall charm, his virtues be revered,
And to his name shall monuments be reared.

SKETCH OF THE TANNAHILL CLUB,

AND THE

ARRANGEMENTS FOR THE CENTENARY CELEBRATION.

ON the Twenty-fifth day of May, Eighteen Hundred and Fifty-eight, a meeting of gentlemen, desirous of commemorating regularly the birth-day of Robert Tannahill, was held in the Globe Hotel, of Paisley. There were present on that occasion—Messrs. James J. Lamb, James Waterston, John Crawford (now the only surviving member), James Motherwell, James Lindsay, and William Pollock. Mr. Lamb was voted to the chair. After many expressions of entire and hearty sympathy with the object for which the meeting was called, it was unanimously agreed "that the meeting resolve itself into

The Tannahill Club,

the special object of which shall be to commemorate, in all time coming, the birthday of Robert Tannahill, who entered this breathing world, whose beauties of scenery he never tired of singing, on the 3rd day of June, 1774."

The constitution adopted for the Club was a simple one :—The anniversary meeting was to be previously advertised, and all who attended were to be held as members of the Club. The gentlemen present at the preliminary meeting were to form a committee to carry out the arrangements for the first anniversary. The chairman for the time to nominate his croupier to be chairman on the following year, and also to appoint the croupier for that year.

The first annual meeting was accordingly held in the Hall of the Saracen's Head Inn, on the evening of Thursday, the 3rd day of June, 1858, since which time the celebration has been regularly held with an amount of enthusiasm which augurs well for the realisation of the word in the constitution of the Club, that it shall be held "in all time coming."

The following is a list of the chairmen of the Club since its commencement :—

1858	...	Mr. James J. Lamb, Architect.
1859	...	„ James Waterston, Editor.
1860	...	„ John Crawford, Writer.
1861	..	„ James Ferrie, Warehouseman.
1862	...	„ Robert L. Henderson, Writer.
1863	...	„ Richard Watson, Editor.
1864	...	„ Robert Cochran, Draper.
1865	...	„ William Fulton, of Glen.
1866	...	„ John Cook, Editor.
1867	...	„ David Campbell, Writer.
1868	...	„ Robert Hay, Lithographer.
1869	...	„ William Stewart, Architect.
1870	...	„ John Fisher, Accountant.
1871	...	„ John S. Mitchell, Boot and Shoe Maker.
1872	...	„ James J. Lamb, Architect.
1873	...	„ James Reid, Bookseller.
1874	...	David Murray, Esq., Banker, Provost of Paisley.

Mr. Lamb, besides occupying the chair on two different occasions, as above stated, was Secretary to the Club from its institution, in 1858, till the year 1870, and from that time till his death, in 1872, he held the office of Honorary Secretary—Mr. James Reid being, since 1870, Acting Secretary.

At the Anniversary Celebration, held in 1873, it was suggested by the Chairman that, as the following year would be the centenary of the birth of Tannahill, the Committee of the Club, with power to add to its number, might be appointed to make arrangements for a banquet or other public entertainment worthy of the occasion, the Provost to be Chairman. This was unanimously agreed to.

Acting on this resolution, a Meeting of Committee of the Tannahill Club was held on Wednesday, 22nd April last, to consider the most appropriate manner of observing the Centenary. Various opinions were expressed as to the form the celebration should assume, and it was considered advisable that a number of the admirers of Tannahill should be invited to confer with the Committee, and assist in making necessary arrangements. With this object in view, it was proposed by the Secretary "that Provost Murray, as Chairman of the Club, be requested to convene a meeting of all interested in the approaching Centenary, and that trades' delegates be specially invited to attend, in order to secure their co-operation in making any arrangements that might be resolved on." The motion was seconded by Councillor Cochran, and unanimously agreed to.

The proposed meeting, convened by the Provost, was held in the Artizans' Institution, on Tuesday, 28th April. A large Committee, representing all classes in the community, was appointed to make the necessary arrangements. The Committee met on the following week, and resolved on a Procession to the "Braes o' Gleniffer," made classic by the muse of Tannahill. They also agreed to hold a Soiree in the evening, at which our Poet's Songs would be sung, and sub-Committees were appointed to carry out the arrangements.

A requisition, largely and influentially signed, was also presented to the Provost, requesting him to call a meeting, to arrange for a Public Banquet. The meeting having been held, it was resolved that the proposed banquet should take the form of a public dinner, to be held in the Abercorn Rooms. The Provost was nominated to preside, and a Committee formed to make the necessary arrangements.

Meantime, the various sub-Committees appointed by the enlarged Committee of the Tannahill Club, set to work enthusiastically. The proposed Procession, as now arranged, will muster some 3000 strong. After marching through the town, it will proceed to Glenfield, where a grand rural *fete* will be held on the plateau above "Tannahill's well." Floral Arches will be erected at prominent points on the route of the procession; and the birthplace of the Poet in Castle Street, as well as his residence and weaving shop, in Queen Street, will be decorated with flowers and evergreens. The proposed Soiree has also assumed a definite form. Accommodation will be provided in the Drill Hall for 1000 persons, presided over by Thomas Coats, Esq., of Ferguslie, a locality hallowed by Tannahill in one of his earliest lyrics—

> Sweet Ferguslie, hail! thou'rt the dear sacred grove,
> Where first my young muse spread her wing;
> Here nature first waked me to rapture and love,
> And taught me her beauties to sing.

At the Soiree, addresses bearing on Tannahill will form a feature in the programme, and his songs will be sung by solo vocalists, as well as by a choir.

Thus will Paisley honour, most appropriately, the birth-day Centenary of one of her most gifted sons, and one of the sweetest singers that Scotland, so rich in sons of song, has produced. Though of humble birth, his fame, like every true son of genius, has gone on increasing with the rolling years; and no doubt need now be entertained of posterity keeping his memory green.

J. B.

PAISLEY, 29th May, 1874.

The centenary of the birth of Robert Tannahill was celebrated in Paisley on the 3rd June, 1874. For a considerable time before active preparations were made to make an *occasion* worthy of the poet, and worthy of the town. A public meeting, held to consider how this could best be done, declared for a holiday and a procession, and a committee was appointed to arrange all details. They set about their work with a will, and when the day arrived it was apparent they had fulfilled the trust to the satisfaction of even the most critical. Seven very fine floral arches were erected at various prominent parts of the town. These cost a very considerable sum, which was defrayed by public subscription. Nor was private enterprise awanting in this direction, many houses being very tastefully decorated with flowers, evergreens, &c. It were invidious to name any, there being hundreds deserving their mead of praise. In fact, it seemed as if the town had suddenly been transformed into a shrubbery. The morning of Wednesday the 3rd found Paisley, therefore, in her "braws." The sound of drums in almost every quarter of the town, and the tramp of hurrying feet, told there was something unusual astir. The various trades in town, as well as the Freemasons, Odd-fellows, &c., and deputies from other places, met in their various *rendezvous*, and marched, headed each by a band, to the place of meeting—St. James' Street—where they were arranged in their ball-lotted order by Captain Sutherland of the burgh police. The number who turned out from the various bodies was very considerable, and their appearance was very pleasing. Perhaps the others will pardon us if we say that the carters really attracted an unusual amount of attention. They turned out to the number of 150, mounted on their chargers, which were decked with ribbons of all the colours of the rainbow, and more—as Paisley and her dyers really can do. There were strong, powerful animals, down to the tiniest *Shelty*, and each one seemed to know it was a holiday. The riders were not less varied—some dressed most fashionably, up to the satin hat, and others wore the broadest *Kilmarnocks* ever Stewarton produced. Truly it was a quaint scene, and will not easily be forgotten. After having paraded the town, they marched to Gleniffer Braes. Mr. Fulton of The Glen not only threw open his grounds and erected some tasteful arches, but actually constructed a road to enable the processionists to gain the Braes in marching order, all which must have cost him a large sum of money. On the summit a platform had been erected, from which a choir, under the leadership of Mr. M'Gibbon, sang various songs of Tannahill's in fine style, and Provost Murray and other gentlemen gave short addresses. The day, which was good, was spent by many in rambling over the Braes, and by others in dancing on the green sward to the music of the bands which were stationed all around, while others thronged the tents to slake their thirst. The order, sobriety, and good conduct, however, of all were the subject of commendation.

In the evening a banquet was held in the Abercorn Rooms—Provost Murray in the chair.

There was also a festival held in the Drill Hall at eight in the evening, presided over by Thomas Coats, Esq. After tea short speeches were delivered, but recitations and the singing of Tannahill's songs were the order of the day. Altogether, a jolly day was spent, and one which, every one affirms, did honour to ourselves, as well as to the memory of our revered and lamented poet.

INDEX.

POEMS.